HIGH BONNET

Idwal Jones

High Bonnet

A Novel of Epicurean Adventures

Ruth Reichl
SERIES EDITOR

Introduction by Anthony Bourdain

THE MODERN LIBRARY

NEW YORK

2001 Modern Library Paperback Edition

Introduction copyright © 2001 by Anthony Bourdain
Series introduction copyright © 2001 by Ruth Reichl

Originally published in hardcover by Prentice-Hall, Inc. in 1945.

LIBRARY OF CONGRESS CATALOGING-IN-PUBLICATION DATA
Jones, Idwal, 1890–1964.
High bonnet: a novel of epicurean adventures / Idwal Jones.
p. cm.—(Modern Library food series)
ISBN 0-375-75756-2
1. Restaurants—Fiction. 2. Young men—Fiction. 3. Cookery—Fiction.
4. Cooks—Fiction. I. Title. II. Modern Library food.
PS3519.O43 H5 2001
813'.52—dc21   00-067901

Modern Library website address: www.modernlibrary.com

Printed in the United States of America

2 4 6 8 9 7 5 3 1

Introduction to the Modern Library Food Series

Ruth Reichl

My parents thought food was boring. This may explain why I began collecting cookbooks when I was very young. But although rebellion initially inspired my collection, economics and my mother's passion fueled it.

My mother was one of those people who found bargains irresistible. This meant she came screeching to a halt whenever she saw a tag sale, flea market, or secondhand store. While she scoured the tables, ever optimistic about finding a Steuben vase with only a small scratch, an overlooked piece of sterling, or even a lost Vermeer, I went off to inspect the cookbooks. In those days nobody was much interested in old cookbooks and you could get just about anything for a dime.

I bought piles of them and brought them home to pore over wonderful old pictures and read elaborate descriptions of dishes I could only imagine. I spent hours with my cookbooks, liking the taste of the words in my mouth as I lovingly repeated the names of exotic sauces: soubise, Mornay, dugléré. These things were never seen around our house.

As my collection grew, my parents became increasingly baffled. "Half of those cookbooks you find so compelling," my mother complained, "are absolutely useless. The recipes are so old you couldn't possibly use them."

How could I make her understand? I was not just reading recipes. To me, the books were filled with ghosts. History books left me cold, but I had only to open an old cookbook to find myself standing in some other place or time. "Listen to this," I said, opening an old tome with suggestions for dinner on a hot summer evening. I read the first recipe, an appetizer made of lemon gelatin poured into a banana skin filled with little banana balls. "When opened, the banana looks like a mammoth yellow pea pod," I concluded triumphantly. "Can you imagine a world in which that sounds like a good idea?" I could. I could put myself in the dining room with its fussy papered walls and hot air. I could see the maid carrying in this masterpiece, hear the exclamations of pleasure from the tightly corseted woman of the house.

But the magic didn't work for Mom; to her this particular doorway to history was closed. So I tried again, choosing something more exotic. "Listen to this," I said, and began reading. "'Wild strawberries were at their peak in the adjacent forests at this particular moment, and we bought baskets of them promiscuously from the picturesque old denizens of the woods who picked them in the early dawn and hawked them from door to door. . . . The pastry was hot and crisp and the whole thing was permeated with a mysterious perfume. . . . Accompanied by a cool Vouvray, . . . these wild strawberry tarts brought an indescribable sense of well-being. . . .'"

"Anything?" I asked. She shook her head.

Once I tried reading a passage from my very favorite old cookbook, a memoir by a famous chef who was raised in a small village in the south of France. In this story he recalls being sent to the butcher when he was a small boy. As I read I was transported to Provence at the end of the nineteenth century. I could see the village with its small stone houses and muddy streets. I could count the loaves of bread lined up at the *boulangerie* and watch the old men hunched over glasses of red wine at the café. I was right there in the kitchen as the boy handed the carefully wrapped morsel of meat to his mother, and I watched her put it into the pot hanging in the big fireplace. It sizzled; it was so real to me that I could actually smell the daube. My mother could not.

But then she was equally baffled by my passion for markets. I could stand for hours in the grocery store watching what people piled into their carts. "I can look through the food," I'd try to explain. "Just by paying attention to what people buy you can tell an awful lot about them." I would stand there, pointing out who was having hard times, who was religious, who lived alone. None of this interested my mother very much, but I found it fascinating.

In time, I came to understand that for people who really love it, food is a lens through which to view the world. For us, the way that people cook and eat, how they set their tables, and the utensils that they use all tell a story. If you choose to pay attention, cooking is an important cultural artifact, an expression of time, place, and personality.

I know hundreds of great cookbooks that deserve to be rescued from oblivion, but the ones I have chosen for the Modern Library Food Series are all very special, for they each offer more than recipes. You can certainly cook from these books, but you can also read through the recipes to the lives behind them. These are books for cooks and armchair cooks, for historians, for people who believe that what people eat—and why—is important.

INTRODUCTION

Anthony Bourdain

The term "foodie" has come to mean someone enthusiastic about, or even preoccupied with, food and restaurants and chefs in particular, a character who exists on the fringes of the restaurant business—either writing about it, dealing with it in some ancillary way as perhaps a wine merchant, food stylist, critic, or consultant might, or simply as an avid observer and regular diner—someone always on the lookout for something new, something marvelous, for the next thing. You might think you know a foodie or two. You don't.

As a chef and student of the history and literature of my profession, I thought I knew all the "chef books." By "chef books," I mean books written about or from the point of view of chefs, works that capture the particular worldview, peculiarities, obsessions, and daily routines of culinary professionals past. As a young prep cook just beginning my long and occasionally painful climb to the top of the kitchen brigade, I came across a tattered copy of Orwell's *Down and Out in Paris and London,* and I can hardly describe the excitement of my discovery, the warm feeling of recognition, the immediate sense of kinship with the *plongeurs* and *cuisiniers* of Orwell's pseudonymous Hotel X. My effort, my anonymous toil in the belly of a large, busy restaurant prep kitchen, was suddenly part of a glorious continuum—the bullying, the insanity, the hard-drinking part of a rich tradition that fortified the hearts and honed the skills of the deserving and weeded out the unworthy—stages in a process to be endured proudly. Early chefs' predilection for alternating unbelievably obscene tirades with withering sarcasm became overnight an art form to be appreciated and emulated—even when I was the hapless target of their scorn. I was, I realized after reading Orwell—and later the work of former chef/mystery author Nicolas Freeling—part of something bigger than myself; I was a soldier in a secret near-paramilitary organization, a soon-to-be made member of an underworld society, a "thing" that had been going on for centuries out of the view of the general public. I had, I realized, without fully understanding it at the time, committed myself to a subculture for whom food revealed its secrets, a debauched elite who worked at different hours, took its pleasures in different ways, and viewed the world outside the kitchen doors and outside the late-night revelries of cooks and chefs with suspicion and dismay. Any book, television show, or movie that opens a window into This Thing of Ours is usually brought immediately to my attention: "Dude!" one of my cook friends will say, "You see that Gordon Ramsey video? He's hard-core, man, you gotta check it out!" or, "You see Al Pacino in *Frankie and Johnny*? Whassup with that neckerchief thing? Man thinks he Chef Boyardee or somethin'! You watch him move back there? I wouldn't hire that goof for a dishwasher!" or "Check out this book *Flash in the Pan*, man! He got it right. It's all there . . ." Chefs are legendary gossips—and the chefs' information network—an informal, worldwide web of kitchen phones, online message boards, late-night bars and e-mails—would impress the CIA or NSA (if they knew about it). A chef hurls a bowl of pasta at a waiter in Seattle, someone hears about it in New York. A lost classic of cuisine is about to be reprinted, somebody, somewhere has already got a full review up on a chef message board—a weathered copy is being passed around from one calloused hand to another. (I've seen more copies of English-language versions of Zola's foodie Dead Sea Scrolls, *The Belly of Paris*, in the last few months than supposedly exist in the country.)

We chefs like reading about ourselves and about our peers, past and present.

Idwal Jones' *High Bonnet* took me by complete surprise. I knew nothing of the book or its author until a galley arrived in the mail, and my reaction—after only a few chapters—was something like outrage. As a chef, I don't like surprises, and Jones' incredible account of lunatic chefs and maniacal gourmands surprised the hell out of me. "Why don't I know about this guy? Who was he? Where did this book come from? Was the author a chef? How much of it is true?" The author had to have been a chef or professional cook—that was without question. But the descriptions of food and cooking were ... well ... nearly pornographic, his accounts of kitchen life so close to the bone. It was a mystery that grew more deliciously painful with each turned page.

High Bonnet is ostensibly the story of Jean-Marie Gallois, the nephew of a *confiseur* from Provence, a young man who from the early pages seems fully imbued with the culinary sensibilities of the Mediterranean. From the get-go, every character seems single-mindedly, almost insanely obsessed with food and wine. Life, in Jones' story, revolves around the getting of food, the cooking of food, the discussion of food—and the planning for same. When Jean-Marie throws together an impromptu Sauce Sicilienne for his uncle and guest—a down-on-her-luck baroness—he finds himself recommended for employment at a prestigious Paris restaurant, the Faisan d'Or. A description of the baroness' reaction to Jean-Marie's sauce illustrates what I mean by pornographic: "The sauce was unlocking memories that her infancy had bequeathed her of Rhone vineyards blinding white in sunshine; Provence with its 'garlic-scented smile'; the buttery in her ancestral kitchen, with its rows of herb canisters; the dry rattle of coriander, as evocative of Egypt as the flutes in *Aïda;* tangerine peel, with its regal pungence and aroma; the butter and chives recalling a tangy cow yard and mossy-walled garden by the Mediterranean shore where she had gathered shells in her pinafore." Whew! I don't know about you, but I need a glass of ice water.

Professional cooks will recognize the intricate hierarchy, familiar character types, and profane dialect of the restaurant kitchen. But even they, I think, will be shocked by the intensity with which all the characters in *High Bonnet* pursue their pleasures and their craft. Everyone, it seems, is a gourmet or a gourmand, racing through life oblivious to all creature comforts but the pursuit of flavor. Cook and aristocrat, Vietnamese anarchist, dwarflike *rôtisseur*, expat Colombian, alcoholic waiter, madman, and hustler alike all careen through Paris' dark arrondissements in search of something good to eat, something wonderful to cook—all of them with strong opinions about food—no sooner finishing one meal than planning another. Meet Jules, the sauce master from the Faisan d'Or who bonds with Jean-Marie, his young charge, over a secret stash of saffron, who refers to Sauce Espagnol, rightly, as "a springboard . . . a mother of all fancies," words that any right-thinking cook can wrap around himself like a warm blanket. There's Pierre, the ugliest but best waiter in Paris, who survives on bread and brandy during working hours to devour the world after. And there's Guido, the "Italian maestro," a classic example of what French cooks refer to as a *debrouillard*, an extricator—that much valued breed of improviser/hustler/spy and artist that all chefs fortunate enough to find keep on their payrolls:

"Guido was from Venice. Venetians make good artists, spies, and historians; Casanova was all three. Guido knew all that was whispered in the Faisan d'Or. . . . Further, he was a geographer, and so learned in the arcana of foods that if you mentioned any point on this revolving globe he could tell you whatever it produced that was edible, and how much it was entitled to respect. . . . Ah, the furious swiftness of our Italian maestro, his flood of awful mediaeval profanity, oaths curling his lips, eyes shining with the gleam of a serpent's! He worked best after he had cursed and lashed himself into a rage." I've known this guy. A few times. Sous-chef material.

Less a story of Jean-Marie's rise to chefdom (when he gets his high bonnet) than a madcap rush to pleasure, the story seems to lose itself to its characters' monomania as it hurtles them along in search of culinary kicks. There is no snobbery in *High Bonnet*. Good food is for those knowledgeable enough and sensitive enough and enthusiastic enough to appreciate it. Whether it's a simple bowl of pasta with "buttery tomato sauce" or a hilarious "Pleistocene Dinner" made from a recently discovered prehistoric musk ox, a classic sauce or, in one priceless moment, a meal of roasted kidneys in a "filthy little café on the banks of a canal . . . noisy, full of tanners and abattoir workmen . . . dogs yelp[ing] underfoot" where "four mastodonic kidneys, whose ruby meat winked in the matrix of fat . . . slid . . . into the stove, to frizzle and snap like Chinese firecrackers," there is no law, only pleasure. For the discerning eater, no rules apply other than the dictates of the palate.

Much of the joy of *High Bonnet* comes with simply allowing the characters to talk, to tell stories, to pontificate, to rail. A story of a chef, a "man ruined by a dish," will stay with me forever, a tale of a man who discovers a recipe for curry in India, enjoys spectacular success re-creating it in Paris, and is then brought down horribly when he runs out of a vital ingredient. More timely, perhaps, in the face of a new wave of chefs who practice their craft in sterile, nearly heat-free *laboratoires*, is a spirited discussion of the appropriate degree of filth in a restaurant kitchen: "Never expect a perfect dinner to emerge from a clean kitchen. As well expect one from a laboratory. Revolting! A cook whose mind runs on soap and antiseptics is fit only for the guillotine," says one character. "Now take Papa Andrieu at the Vielle Tour. His little kitchen is about four feet by ten. If its floor were trimmed with a pick and shovel—which Heaven forbid!—the ceiling would be very much higher. It is an Alps of peelings, cinders, grease, impacted chicken bones, and bread. The debris of meals goes back to the days of the War—perhaps the Napoleonic Wars! . . . Assuredly, where vision and creative flame exist, a little honest dirt is no barrier to art."

Spoken like many an old-school professional, I'm afraid.

When I finally found a brief biography of *High Bonnet*'s author, Idwal Jones, I was, if anything, more tantalized. He was, it appears, something of a renaissance man; authoring works of criticism, Western fiction, viticulture, folklore, and cooking. He worked, at various times, as an engineer, prospector, rancher, and journalist, as well as being a Cordon Bleu chef and member of various food and wine societies. A friend of both M.F.K. Fisher and Eric von Stro-heim, he sounds like one fascinating dude. All I can say is he writes like a cook. His book *High Bonnet*, now finally reprinted by Modern Library, will endure as a classic of its genre, food-spattered copies, no doubt, to circulate in many restaurant kitchens. For me, that's the highest praise there is.

———

ANTHONY BOURDAIN is a twenty-eight-year veteran of professional kitchens, having served as a chef, sous-chef, saucier, line cook, prep drone, and dishwasher. A graduate of the Culinary Institute of America, he is currently the executive chef of the brasserie Les Halles in New York City. He is the author of two novels, *Bone in the Throat* and *Gone Bamboo*, and most recently, *Kitchen Confidential: Adventures in the Culinary Underbelly*, a nonfiction account of life in a restaurant kitchen.

CONTENTS

Introduction to the Modern Library Food Series by Ruth Reichl　　vii

Introduction by Anthony Bourdain　　xi

I. IT WAS THE MEDLARS　　3

II. THE GENTLEMAN UPSTAIRS　　16

III. IN PETIT-MONTROUGE　　27

IV. MONSIEUR POM-POM　　38

V. THE DURUY MASK　　50

VI. THE BISHOP'S ARBOR　　59

VII. CHEFS DINE ELSEWHERE　　67

VIII. MANUEL, THE INCA　　75

IX. MAYOR IN THE ATTIC　　83

X. FRANÇOIS LE GRAND　　88

XI. MUSK OX AND SHERBET　　96

XII. FROM OVERSEAS　　108

XIII. TINKERS' HOLIDAY　　118

XIV. LORDS AND LADIES, *VALE!*　　126

PUPIL: Good Master, many men have written largely on cookery; so either prove you're saying something original, or else don't tease me.

COOK: What I know I didn't learn in a brace of years, wearing the apron just by way of sport!

—Athenæus: *Banquet of the Learned*

HIGH BONNET

It Was the Medlars

The vender was again passing Xavier's café on the Toulon wharf with a basket of medlars on his head, a tuneful cry in his throat. The season being advanced, the fruit was dark-gold, pulpy, deliciously overripe.

"On this voyage to Genoa, Jean-Marie," the master of the *Piccolo* was saying, as he filled my glass, "you will be first officer. *Bene?*"

It was high rank for a youth just turned eighteen. The master was a Sicilian, gravely kind, with the petrel's luck in a hurricane, and he had taught me to navigate by thumb, eye, and quadrant. No longer was I a cabin boy. I could now tread the deck of the *Piccolo* with a franc's worth of gilt on my cap. There she was at her berth, rocking and jouncing in the tail end of a mistral, trim in the bright sunlight, and reeking of oil, wine barrels, and the woodsy smell of cork.

The vender sang out his wares. The wind came laden with the odor of them, and I thought of the medlar tree in my uncle's garden, and fell a-longing.

"For a day or two I should like to be home." I pointed. "That fruit—"

The master turned his head. "Medlars! And it is April already!" With elbows on the table he cupped his stubbled blue jowl in his hands and sighed dreamily, staring at the basket. "And at Palermo the old Suora Micaela goes crying her medlars. *'Nespole! Che belle nespole!'* Ah, the indigo sea of the Concha d'Oro, and the sherbet we bought at the carts to eat with the Suora's fruit!"

The next minute we were eating medlars, which is an art when done properly. You pinch off the bud, gouge down to the seeds, then tear away the peel, and pop the medlar into your mouth. The three lucent seeds drop out easily like bullets. And you wash the pulp down with a gulp of Muscatel that bears the Tuscan mark on a black label.

By the time we had finished, the wharf and the *Piccolo* were wrapped in blackness, and fat Xavier in his cave back of the shop was fusing oil and wine in a great burst of flames. The incense of saffron was as magisterial as a fugue played on brass sirens. Xavier waddled over to us with the dish. Since it included young lobsters from the Porquerolles, and a good-sized *rascasse,* we prolonged our dinner until midnight.

"The next voyage, then," said the master when he saw me off on the autobus for the mountains above Nice.

"To the next!"

"Addio!"

The vast Ajax-like arm that had conquered storms on the Mediterranean sketched a wobbly farewell in the obscurity of the arch. And Xavier, like a wine tun swathed in a sheet, waved a farewell like a benediction, as well he might, for I had spent a month's wages.

I never returned to the sea, nor ever saw the *Piccolo* again. It was the medlars.

————

My Uncle Abel was a *confiseur,* and I owned a tiny share in his concern—a bequest of my father, who had run through the rest of his inheritance before he joined the Foreign Legion and was lost in some Saharan combat. Abel's *nougat* was one of the enduring memorials of Vence, a hill town renowned also for its panorama and its moteless air, which has the purity of crystal.

His shop was a cavern in the Rue Miséricorde. Its windows were densely veiled with cobwebs, but from the door one could see Le Mounier, the soaring icicle Du Cheiron, and Caire Gros, frozen as it tried to stab heaven with its rose-azure spears.

The town is of Romanesque archways, high rubble buildings, Ligurian towers built in the arrogant style of the Genoese cinquecento; the houses are of pink and ocher stucco, their harshness softened by time, the mistral, and the corroding fogs from the sea.

Near by winds a stream in which dwell trout, carp, dace, and tench, with sage and mint growing on the banks. You can hook a fish there, then fling back and lodge it in the kitchen of Mère Solon's tavern. This is a legend that brought many sportsmen to the tavern and made Mère Solon rich, but only three times was the feat performed.

My uncle once did better, and won a fifty-franc bet at the tobacconist's. He turned, as on a pivot, flicked a trout through the air, through the door, and splash into a pot of *court-bouillon* bubbling on the fire!

By the time he had walked to the tavern, his dish of *truite au bleu* was smoking for him on the table, with a salad done in Mère Solon's best vein, and a bottle of white Cavalaire, a gift to the champion fly caster of Vence.

Or should I say the universe? Yes, assuredly the universe. It was rather a small fish, hardly a mouthful for my uncle, but inside of a fortnight it was said in Nice the trout weighed six pounds, and that my uncle had cast it into the pot from across the river.

"Que diable!" said he. "How could I remember? I have caught and eaten twenty fish since then!"

The very next month, the elections were to be held. Why not, asked many citizens, why not put up Abel Gallois for mayor? Why not, indeed? His fame was resounding. The trouble was, every party—Leftist, Centrist, Rightist—had already selected its candidate. Besides, M. Gallois was anti-Clerical and an Anarchist, the sole Anarchist in the village. Etienne Dosso, the wine cooper, said the honor had somehow to be conferred, and that, since there was no Royalist party on the rolls, why not assemble one? It was done, and my uncle, his protests being set down to modesty, was elected mayor by a majority nothing short of staggering.

A man of ability, the philosophers tell us, can apply his energy in any direction. They were wrong in this instance. As an angler my uncle had talent; as a nougat maker he had genius of a high order; as a statesman he displayed only mediocre gifts, though his bulk and portentous roar were like nothing since Mirabeau. But *noblesse oblige,* and he was a patriot. From head to foot he equipped himself with the habiliments of mayor—silk hat, frock coat, sash, and staff—at the cost of two thousand francs, and on Bastille Day closed his shop, and paraded in lone dignity through the village, magnificent, yet humble in spirit, visiting the remotest lane on the hillside, so that the indigent old gooseherds might view passing over their own doorstep the symbol and personification of the Republic.

His affairs did not suffer from this devotion to the labors of office. Visitors came up by the hundreds, and the Syndicat had an enormous sign, paid for by the electors, hung over the front of the shop, and it was carved out in the shape of a bouquet, with the legend: "Homage from the World to Nougat Masséna, and Abel Gallois, King of Confectioners."

As with M. Antoine Carême, whose dinners as chef to Talleyrand rendered the Congress of Vienna so memorable in diplomatic history, sugar was my uncle's outlet for expression. True, gifts were bestowed upon him with an uneven hand. With roulette, the little horses, and rouge-et-noir he had inferior luck. It was a pity! He would go to Nice every two weeks, sometimes with Dosso, the wine cooper, and the Baroness from the hotel, mad gamblers all, and return, strapped, but bragging.

He was gone again when I arrived home. The mimosa trees were beautiful, their yellow *paniches* like hard yolks pressed through a sieve. The medlar trees were plucked; I should have known what to expect, with my uncle within reach of a ripe one.

I pried open the back window and crawled into the shop.

It was silent, the temple of the Nougat Masséna—a vast crypt, dusty-white with starch, its rafters looped with snowy cobwebs as large as sails, as enduring and broomproof as if woven of silver, hanging over the racked tables like drapes on a catafalque.

In the dimness where one could see little, in a silence that was complete except for the doves on the roof tiles, the olfactory nerves were the one channel to the senses. It was a fragrance of citron, almond, honey, ratafia, pistachio, apricot, kirsch, and vanilla, entrancing in its subtlety, no one perfume keyed above the rest; it was Oriental, yet simple and familiar, like the vision of an Ouled-Nail girl dancing on sweet fern.

The other room, paved with slabs, had a range sunk into the wall, table and chairs, and a large disordered cot.

I leaned out the front window. An apprentice was ringing mallet on hoops before Dosso's shop. Farther down, the gendarmes were before their office, twisting their mustaches and talking with the extreme importance of gendarmes in a village where nothing ever happens. At the other end of the street was the hotel.

It was pretty hollow now, Vence, with my uncle, Dosso the wine cooper, and the Baroness gone. The two men were twins in girth, exuberance, and digestive powers. The Baroness, an English lady, was their pet, their mascot at the casino. She was a blowsily plenteous woman, weighing not an ounce less than three hundred pounds, with the jolliest laugh in Vence. Her income was minute, barely enough to keep the average British spinster in tea and caraway buns. She expanded it by painting crags and trees, thumping hard on the canvas with thumb and palette knife. *"Pointillisme—c'est de la boue!"* It was muck, but it was stuff that sold.

Twice a month she arrayed herself in court robes—those welltended vestiges of her former grandeur—balanced a paste tiara on her head, and rode down to the casino at Nice. It was all or nothing when the Baroness played at baccarat.

Sometimes she left her tiara at the pawnshop, but she observed her return with a repast that seldom varied. She dined, this prodigal daughter, on a plate of red mullets; toadstools cooked in cream; a grouse with orange sauce, and stuffed artichoke hearts à la Mornay; an herb salad; then a flan, or a Grand Marnièr *bombe,* with Ven-

tadour cheese and a plate of cherries. Burgunday always followed
along, two bottles, and then a cup of Armagnac to seal the palate
with dryness.

Her jests and booming laughter fanned the windows like the
mistral. The landlady and the staff adored her. That amorphous
bulk, crowned with the tiara, cast luster upon the hotel and was,
after the *nougat*, the town's chief pride.

The Armagnac gone to the last drop, her eyes glazing, she held a
cigarette to her lips. That was her ritual. She had the true gourmand's distrust of tobacco. She smoked only as a penance, and to
correct any slight tendency to excess at the board. After three or
four puffs her opulent forearm, like a sack of semiliqueous fat,
looped delicately at the bangled wrist, fell; the Baroness was asleep.

That was the signal for the landlady to call down the street:
"M'sieu Abel! M'sieu Dosso!"

And that in turn brought the cooper and my uncle up on the trot,
and they carried the Baroness upstairs to her room.

If Dosso was drunk, or playing cards at the tavern, and my uncle
was intent over his boiling sirup, with eyes glued to the thermometer, help was got elsewhere. The little gendarmes came up sedately,
hatless, taking long breaths to collect strength for the task ahead of
them.

It took maneuvering to lift themselves upright, with the
Baroness on their heads, and grope their way to the stairs. Nothing
of them was visible under that mammoth bulk in black silk, as
shapeless as a cloud, except their quaking legs, which seemed always on the verge of snapping like pipestems. It was a relief to the
watchers in the hallway when the group, like a four-legged monster,
tottered into the front room, and a thud assured them that finally
the Baroness was on her bed.

The gendarmes came down triumphant but fatigued, and got a
tumbler of *marc* apiece for their pains. We sipped it—I got my share
for carrying up the tiara—at the abandoned table, men privileged
to be in the service of the second most illustrious person in Vence.

"Hey! What cheese!" mumbled the older gendarme, trying some
on a cracker. "Ventadour?"

"Well, not quite." Madame's eyes were limpid with trouble. "It's Thome de Savoie, aged in brandy. Ah, if she finds out, will I ever hear the end of it!"

As it was, she heard nothing but praise. The Baroness had a large, tolerant heart, and her kindness was infinite. I am grateful to her. She insisted on talking with me in English.

———

It was pitch-dark, with a gale thrumming at the tiles, and lashings of rain. My uncle crashed in first, soaked and blown, but with breath enough to give me a torrential welcome. Then a clasp from the valiant Dosso, all but unrecognizable in tie and coat, for the casino demands the last punctilio of elegance; and then the hand of the majestic Baroness to kiss.

"Not a soldo left!" bellowed my uncle. "A great night! So, Dosso?"

"Formidable!"

They flung off their wrappings. We built a fire, dragged up some chairs, and had a round of brash, red Niçois wine.

"I brought them here for dinner," said my uncle. "And what have we got?"

He peered into the cupboard, into a meat safe hanging outside the back door, and into some musty sacks under the sink—nothing more than a loaf of bread and a pint of veal-knuckle soup in a casserole! Dosso roared as he stretched himself out in his chair and smacked his thigh. The Baroness, despite her famished state, smiled with wan yet unconquerable hope.

"Given the material—pullets, and so forth—anyone can make a dinner. But from nothing—ah, you watch me! I think I have some *pâté* in here."

He went into the crypt, and we shadowed him as he made his search. The perfume of the *nougat* was still full, still entrancing. My uncle pried cubes from the rack molds, ratafia nougats, fine samples of his craft, blooming with a peach-like *duvet*.

"Taste them."

"Perfect!"

"More. Taste the pistachios this time."

"Admirable!"

"Mustapha's prime." My uncle brayed a pistachio in his palm and waved it under Dosso's nose. "Oily and green. The most delicate hint of terebinth."

"Away with it!" bellowed Dosso, recoiling. "Poison!"

The Baroness sniffed at it faintly, and remarked it was pleasant. My uncle loudly began to champion his pistachios.

What was any perfume to Dosso and the Baroness, wet and ravenous, who would have sold Mustapha and his orchard, and thrown in all Egypt, for a thick steak?

I tightened my belt, left all that tragicomedy behind, and sped through the rain to the grocer's. Its shutters were up. The hotel was a black tomb. A café was open, and after much pleading I was allowed to buy a saucer of liver paste, a lettuce, and two withered tangerines.

As I hurried back over the cobbles, half strangled in the gale, a phalanx of geese came charging up the narrow alley. Roughed by the wind, they were in vexed humor, squalling like mad—a lost herd, possibly from Ventadour or Sospel. As well meet a gang of Apaches! In a doorway I stood as flat as a poster whilst they squalled past, heads thrust out, wings thundering, looking like so many hurtling tenpins. They numbered two hundred, at least, for I stood counting by the light of the alley lamp as pints of water coursed down my neck.

I saw my chance and hurried on, just as the rearguard espied me. A goose may be erratic, but it is never dense. Loathing discomfort, as sybaritic as a peacock or a swan, it prefers a warm shelter to a hammering in a gale. The entire phalanx clamored about me, waist-high, smiting with their beaks and wings as hard as shutters, taking me for the cause of their misfortunes. I fought to the door and wriggled in. My uncle peered out, astonished, into a blizzard of feathers.

"The hook! The hook—in Heaven's name!"

He thrust the pothook into the night, and pulled in a vast, fighting harpy of a goose, larger than a condor. It stilled, and then it got tossed into Dosso's embrace; he stood guffawing mightily, patting its bosom. He plucked it, flashed an inch-long blade, and in small time all that was potentially edible of the goose quit its skeleton. Into a copper saucepan it went, then into the oven, for Dosso had stoked up a roaring fire.

"*Croustades,* Abel—heh?"

My uncle mixed and baked four deep little trays of puff paste. The Baroness tore the lettuce and shook up a dressing of ropy oil and tart apricot juice. In the reverberating oven, a private inferno, the goose crackled under the spooned unguent of wine, herbs, condiments, and tangerine essence. That was my task, to drip the unguent on its glazed breast.

As in a trance, I being famished, and the odors throwing me back to a little water-front eating place in Valencia famous for its baked fowl and sauces, I added a fat pinch of bitter chocolate. And I had learned a thing or two aboard the *Piccolo*! I boiled down a pitcher of the veal stock with the unguent, tangerine peel, a bulb of garlic, and a nip of coriander, and allied it with *roux.*

"*Gaudeamus igitur—*" rolled my uncle's voice with lusty splendor in the rafters. He wore a purple shirt with arm bands of flounced ribbon, a yellow belt and yellower shoes; in bulk and face he resembled Dumas.

Plates rang on the bleached pine table; wine gurgled into the tumblers. I laid segments of the bird in the *croustades,* covered them with the sauce, and slid a helping before each.

Bus-riding, gambling, and cooking had stayed us from nutriment so long that we were voracious. Dosso bit first.

"Ah!"

It was such a cry as would be wrenched from an old peasant woman at her first pyrotechnic display, seeing a remote ball of fire, so high in the velvety heavens that it couldn't mount farther, lip out a delicious burst of stars.

We ate steadily, with condonable grossness; in silence, save for the champing of Dosso's mastiff jaws and the click of the lady's rings on her tumbler. It was the instinctive silence of gourmands.

There is often a jealousy between our senses, which so often hinder one another; and they are the more envious the more highly they are trained. Discourse, however witty and brief, would have been out of place. Montaigne speaks of the ill custom of popular and base men, who call for minstrels or singers at table, whereas men of concept and understanding abhor such boorish distraction. Alcibiades, a man exquisitely skillful at making good cheer, prohibited even a distant flute at the place of feasting.

The Baroness ate with eyes half drooped, like a pigeon's in flight, allowing the *croustade* to splinter under her excellent teeth. She dabbed with lumps of bread and pushed them, dripping with sauce, into her mouth in absorption, as if listening to the orchestration of flavors echoing against the soundingboard of her palate.

The sauce was unlocking memories that her infancy had bequeathed her of Rhone vineyards blinding white in sunshine; Provence with its "garlic-scented smile"; the buttery in her ancestral kitchen, with its rows of herb canisters; the dry rattle of coriander, as evocative of Egypt as the flutes in *Aïda*; tangerine peel, with its regal pungence and aroma; the butter and chives recalling a tangy cow yard and mossy-walled garden by the Mediterranean shore where she had gathered shells into her pinafore.

The bird eaten, we pushed aside our plates. The salad bridged the gap to the wine, the oil clearing the tongue, the apricot juice a corrective for the taste buds. Then we drank wine.

My uncle drank precisely three times at a dinner—before it, during, and after. He drank a bottleful each time. If by accident he exceeded the limit, then, as if not to offend the rule of Democritus—of whom he could never have heard—who forbade us to stay at four as an unlucky number, he went on, if the company was good, to five or six.

Dosso regarded the ceiling tenderly.

"Abel, perhaps—a little coffee, ha?"

He bruised orange peel, spices, and sugar in a bowl, poured on cognac and set it ablaze. My uncle extinguished it with ink-black coffee, and the cups were ladled full. We all four lighted cheroots, our mood being too profound for the triviality of cigarettes. The Baroness seemed wholly asleep, but her fingers were awake, and deftly flicked the band off her cheroot. Talk oozed out in drowsy rills, agreeable to listen to, and profitable to the spirit.

"Monday," said Dosso, "there'll be a Ventadour steer, fattened on heath, at the abattoir. I'll fetch you a steak as big around as this table." He held out his fist. "And that thick. We'll grill it in an armour of rock salt, and break it off with a mallet. At my place."

All eyes gleamed through the murk of repletion. If bodies were rendered dull, brains were clear enough to cope with the pure aesthetic idea.

"That goose," my uncle breathed suddenly. "Whose goose it was, I don't know. I'll find out from the gendarmes in the morning. So fat it was, perhaps Mère Peyrault of Sospel was the owner. I'll send her a box of nougats. Two boxes."

"Three," murmured Dosso. "Geese are up a little, I think. Or perhaps down. I don't know."

The Baroness folded her jewelled fingers on her lap and talked in slow competence, words releasing themselves with each puff from her cheroot.

"Those tangerines," she was saying. "Where else can such ripen, but in the hot afternoons of the Midi? I am very fond of them. Enormously. I like best those from around Hyères.

"I was there one summer, long ago, having the soup at that little restaurant with the palms in front. All at once, I became aware that a change had come over the soup, after ten years. I called over the proprietor.

" 'My compliments,' I told him. 'You have a new cook. She is an artist. Such a delicate, ethereal flavor—of—is it citron, or what?'

" 'But no, madame,' he said. 'The same cook—the same soup, I assure you. Still, it is a flattery.' He bowed, and left."

"Perhaps Madame la Baronne was in love again," boomed my uncle.

"Not that time," drowsed the Baroness, unperturbed. "I had all my senses about me. I turned. And there, next to me, was the mayor, reading a journal propped before him on the table, and eating his dessert. Tangerines. Little ones, that he broke open one by one and munched, peel and all. The voluptuary! In breaking they yielded their oil in a fine vapor. A distillation as far-reaching as ether. They scented his whiskers, in which the ribbons of his pince-nez were caught; they scented the air; they had scented my *potage*."

"It was deliberate," grumbled Dosso. "He was in love with you, and wished to foster your happiness."

"Regardless," she went on. "It is my custom now never to take *potage* without first rubbing my thumb with a tangerine."

My uncle waddled paunchily to bring over the demijohn. It was rough native wine, as honest as sunlight, and with no more pretensions than himself.

———

I learned from him there is much nonsense about wine. Wine is not a thing to be talked about merely, or to sell, or for *littérateurs* to rouse envy and dismay by rattling off a litany of strange and purple nomenclature; but something to enjoy and pour down your throat, with the least ado possible, as if it were fully worthy of you. And the best wine for a man is that grown in his own vineyard or his neighbor's, the blood of his own native soil.

Wine should not be sent away like an unwanted child. Travel ruins wine as it does men. Something of their native virtue and bloom and rootedness goes out of them. Wine, like man, is a living entity, and most congruous where it was bred. It should stay at home. . . .

———

"Three pounds of nougat," my uncle repeated. "The goose was worth it."

"Four," said Dosso, wiping a trickle of wine from his chin.

The Baroness groped for her cheroot as she awoke. She regarded me with a faint smile on her handsome, thoughtful face, and gave two nods of decision, as if she had not been sleeping all the while but cogitating.

"That," she said, "was a Sauce Sicilienne, was it not?"

"Yes, madame."

"It was faultless. It enhanced to an extraordinary degree the quality of a roast bird that was in itself perfect."

I was overwhelmed. Never before had Madame la Baronne, in our hearing, commended a dish, however much it had pleased her.

"You must go to the great kitchens and begin your training to be a *chef de cuisine*. I will give you letters."

"But the *Piccolo* is waiting."

Said my uncle: "Damn the *Piccolo!*"

Destiny itself had spoken with a tone unmistakable in its finality.

"We will celebrate with steaks on Monday," said Dosso.

My uncle nodded. "I will make it four pounds of nougat after all," he said.

II

THE GENTLEMAN UPSTAIRS

The Faisan d'Or had been a priory once, then the palace of a silversmith, then a college for the military. Its salons were echoes of Versailles. The kitchen was distinguished: a vast chancel, the granite walls begrimed with smoke from ten thousand lordly feasts, the aisle a channel of blue haze through which the cooks and apprentices moved like sacristans and acolytes. From the ranges, charcoal gridirons, and rows of copper pots, burnished like altar vessels, incense lifted to the soot-hung louvre overhead.

Here, great chefs had plied their art with cumulative renown for many decades until, through whim, they retired at seventy-five or eighty. Age is little perceived by those who dwell amid pomp and the changeless memorials of eternity. The sacerdotal environment fosters length of years. As a kitchen it was old when Catherine de' Medici, with her retinue of chefs, adepts in pastry, architects in sugar, and vintners, came into Paris—an invasion as epochal as the entry of the Normans into England and the Moguls into Delhi. In retrospect, so few invasions, if naught is destroyed, are to be deplored by the thoughtful. Catherine destroyed nothing. Her cooks worked a catalysis. Instantly, from a noble and existent base of culture, the cuisine of France, her lasting glory, sprang into flower.

Here Richelieu had visited, to watch the beating of a mayonnaise. Over by the high, tinted oriel window, the thoughtful Vatel had stood, brow on hand, meditating before he launched into a delighted world the sauce which, under the name of Sauce Colbert, has ever since been allied with turbot. Under a stag's head on the wall hung a painting, dark as if under a patina of meat glaze, of Béchamel, the inventor of the white sauce that bears his name— one of the enduring souvenirs of Louis XIV's moderately sunny reign.

It was into this cultural heritage that I was pitched, to be deafened by shouts and roasted by the heat of a range as I stirred a large pot with a paddle. For days I did nothing but stir that pot. It held gallons and gallons of stock to be boiled down thick, as a base for Sauce Espagnol. There were four of us sauce apprentices, under the eye of Jules, a little man with rakish toque and a waxed mustache, eternally on the trot, like a fox terrier. Jules, though of no rank in the Faisan d'Or's hierarchy of chefs, was the master of sauces, and monitor of the workers at the ranges. He reminded me of a dog I had once owned.

"Hello," he would say, stopping in his trot. "Now, what was that—*hein?*"

He would sniff, weave back through a tangle of scents, and, as if by feeling along an invisible thread, arrive at a pot that was boiling away like a geyser.

"Stock for *velouté,* eh?" He would sniff again. "A few more carrots, little one. Just a handful."

Then he would trot off again, adjusting a gas cock here and there, turning around the handle of a pan, jabbing a finger into a pot, to give it a lick with the verdict of a nod or a grunt. He was amiable and kind-hearted, this little Provençal, so lost and homesick in Paris that he hardly ever went out evenings, save to talk with friends once a week or so at a café in the Rue de Bac. He slept on a couch in the office, and there passed his spare time, reading papers, smoking temperately, and playing chess by himself. He warmed to me at once as a fellow provincial.

"Look at this!" He unscrewed the top of a brass cartridge and held it to my nose. It was saffron, with an aroma so pungent it froze my olfactory nerves. "Smell! Smell that!"

"Very strong." I could say no more.

"And good!" He stowed his treasure with a wink. "From my home in St.-Rémy! Only one garden grows such a saffron. Not a word to a soul. Not even to Urbain!"

None but myself knew the clue to the grandeur of his Sauce Jules, with its base of game and Espagnol, mélange of claret, mace, thyme, bitter orange, and a whiff of that hidden garden at St.-Rémy. He exulted in the possession of a secret that was inviolably his, that pampered his one grain of egoism. The little Provençal had something wrong with his luck. He had energy, a nose of phenomenal delicacy, a repertory of four hundred sauces and a hundred garnishes that he could mix instantly without looking into his vade mecum, but he had not the political instinct. In any profession it is not often the virtuoso but always the *arriviste*, the wire puller, who attains to high post and wealth. He was a fanatic collector of herbs—sweet Cicely, flag, burnet, cumin, from the Rhine, which he grew outside, below Vatel's window, and a hundred more herbs that lay in envelopes in his cabinet. Epicures like Melun-Perret, the financier, and the Duca di Valmonte, were the gainers by his mania.

Jules was redolent. The petals in that brass cartridge had sent forth an essence that permeated, radium-like, his entire frame. I was conscious of that perfume at the end of my first week. Another poke in my ribs, a chuckle, and I knew Jules was behind me.

"Sssss!" A whisper prefaced all his remarks. "I think—yes, by Heaven, I'll make a *saucier* of you!"

So for another month I piously stirred the pot of Espagnol stock, but I knew what was in it. I threw into it lumps of beef, ham, and veal, fried brown with the hammered bones; roast-fowl carcasses, tomatoes, turnips, onions, carrots, bay leaves, pepper, and all-spice; celery, thyme, marjoram and savory, chervil—and a pinch of the Savoy coriander, a little refinement of Jules'—and kept it at a simmer for a day. After an integration with sherry, it was passed through a hair sieve. And there was the Espagnol pot!

"*Voilà!*" Jules would say. "A springboard, a mother of fancies!"

Just as at Beynac's academy the old lecturer used to declare that the skull was a basal form in art. Draw or model the skull to perfection, and what more can you be taught? The countless expressions of the portraitist you may then lay on at your whim. And this pot was the skull in our cuisine.

Under Jules' tutelage I forayed from the Espagnol pot to such modifications of it as the Chevreuil, Tortue, Genoise, Colbert, and Béyrout, and the marvelous Regency. The good Jules, how patient he was! How wise in his calling! His sensory equipment was flawless. He could tell by the aroma of a roasting joint how much longer it should tarry in the oven. Thrusting his hand into the oven, he could tell with the accuracy of a thermometer the degree of heat, by the sharpness of the pain at the base of the fingernails.

After I had mastered the Espagnol and its variants, I was coached through the *velouté* and the *Béchamel*. Then I came to the end of my probationary three months and was summoned to the presence of Monsieur Paul, the *chef des cuisines*. I trembled. Jules gave me a cuff on the ear.

"Go!" he said sharply.

The hand that pushed me through the door of the sanctum was his. For the first time I beheld the illustrious, the fabled Paul Watier, Chevalier de la Légion d'Honneur. My feelings were those of an apprentice verger gazing upon the Pope. Monsieur Paul rarely moved into the kitchen. His eyes and ears, a telepathic sense, and the whispers of his lieutenants acquainted him with all that transpired in that outer world, as if the wall between his long mahogany desk and the battery of ranges were of glass.

"Gallois?" he asked in a crisp, melodious voice, holding a letter before him.

"Yes, Monsieur."

"Ah!"

He gave me a flashing glance, no longer than a second, then turned sideways, resting his chin upon his hand, and read the letter over again, reverently.

His toque was extraordinarily high, white and starched, ironed by the most skillful of *blanchisseuses*. The whiteness of his coat and full, knotted neckband emphasized the pallor of his rounded, dimpled countenance and the luster of his limpid brown eyes. It was the face of the pure intellectual, but the firmness of the lower lip, though it was moist and cherry-red, the lip of the gourmet, betokened decision. He had the nervous hands of a violinist, rather small, and his carriage, as he sat upright in his chair, his pose, and exalted smooth brow reminded me of the statue of the poet Théodore de Banville in a leafy corner of the Rue Vaugirard. Monsieur Paul had erudition in his craft and a knowledge of art and the classics. His endowment was an exquisite palate, curious yet austere, and so edged that it could cleave through a strange dish and its complexities to the intent of the chef, as swiftly as a yataghan to the heart of a melon.

His antecedents were worthy of his lofty post, for he had served his apprenticeship at Prunier's, and had been coached by his father, a maître d'hôtel at the old Restaurant Noel-Peters, and a novice there before the Franco-Prussian War when Homard à l'Américaine was introduced.

"I have here a letter from Madame la Baronne. A friend, it is evident, of M. Gustave Urbain, our proprietor. It is an honor, I assure you. Madame enjoys high esteem at the Faisan d'Or."

"Monsieur, if you will kindly allow me to say so, I have often heard Madame speak of the Faisan d'Or with admiration."

A flush swept over the ivory pallor of his cheeks. He was touched and deeply gratified. He waved his hand as if modestly diverting the compliment to the house.

"The Faisan d'Or appreciates it—" And then he spoke of other palates of the first rank—Ali Bab, Prosper Montagné, Cournonsky, Bichet-Lévy, chairman of the Réunion des Gastronomes, the adventurous young Paul Reboux, and a dozen other names.

"Madame says—" the letter again crackled, the five lavender sheets of expensive paper, scrawled over loosely at the rate of ten words to the page—"Madame says you achieved *something*—in the way of a Sauce Sicilienne that she *seemingly* approves.

"In which case, you will be taken off the sauces as a finished student. You are now, M'sieu, promoted to the vegetables!"

He pressed a button on his desk. Jules appeared at the first tinkle, his eyes snapping.

"Your pupil goes to the legumes, Monsieur Jules. At your recommendation and that of Madame la Baronne. I think you recall her."

"Very well, sir."

"I think Madame was here last five—or was it six—"

"If I may be permitted, sir, it was the autumn of the year in which Monsieur Melun-Perret abandoned Sauce Batalane for Sauce à la Périgeux with his stuffed legs of partridge. That was four years ago, with your pardon, sir."

Monsieur Paul inclined his high bonnet graciously, thought a moment, then pulled a gourd from the drawer of his desk—a little gourd painted with crude Indian designs. He rattled it delicately at his ear.

"Peppercorns, Monsieur Jules, from Guatemala. This came just in time. I believe that Monsieur Melun-Perret dines tonight, and on ptarmigan? Good! The maître d'hôtel will grind it at his table."

Jules bowed, with a tiny sniff of delight. Monsieur Paul smiled wanly, and went on, "Yes, tonight ptarmigan, à la Duchesse, glazed." A shade of reproach, or perhaps insinuation, had crept into his voice, and his large brown eyes rested indulgently on Jules, as he remarked softly, "It is a cat's age, a *cat's* age, since *I* have tasted ptarmigan."

"With the bird Monsieur Melun-Perret will have flageolets and *pommes* Sarah Bernhardt," Jules said imperturbably. "And Chambertin, 1911."

He opened the gourd, rubbed a peppercorn between his thumb and finger, and sniffed the aroma. His eyelids fluttered. "Good," he remarked, and with a bow he left the room.

Monsieur Paul rubbed his chin briskly, and felt with delicacy to find the balance of his incredible high bonnet.

"Gallois," he said, "you are accepted. And now a word or two for your benefit, young man. You have embarked upon an art that exacts of its devotees the utmost diligence, studious application, a large share of intellect, and the happiest co-ordination of eye and hand."

He stared sternly at me, and I tried not to gulp like a yokel at my tight throat.

"You will matriculate from vegetables, Gallois. Then you will be advanced to fish. I congratulate you in advance: fish is primordial, and a challenge to the artist. Anaximander the wise Greek ascribed a fish origin to man—and yet how few of us can rise to cope worthily with this interesting animal! And none may, Gallois, except those who have passed through the anteroom of the master *saucier.* Matelote, Vénétienne, Allemande for the carp; à la Turque, Horly, Cardinal, Aurora, Portugaise for flounders, plaice, and so forth.

"And, remember!" He lifted a finger. "Always at the Faisan d'Or the strictest sobriety and punctuality!"

I returned to the kitchen. Two score of faces turned upon me like moons. Even the scullions paused, with dripping hands lifted above the suds. Jules walked down with me proudly. He presented me to the trim, saturnine Guido, the vegetable chef.

"Monsieur Gallois, who will assist you. A friend of Monsieur Urbain." (This was true only in a one-sided epistolary sense, for the Baroness' letter had been sent to the proprietor, whom I had not seen.) "And a friend of Madame la Baronne."

Guido bit into an asparagus and shrugged.

"*Quella grande bagascia!* That harlot!"

"She has taste, all the same," returned Jules.

———

Jules was preparing the dinner. The viands for M. Melun-Perret were *"de qualité et de choix."* He was to dine alone tonight. He wished no distraction. Already, in the small Louis XIV chamber, with its thick Chinese carpet, a Gobelin, two Fragonards, and a Corot on the walls, he was sipping his Amontillado. Urbain himself had arranged the settings. M. Melun-Perret, whose midriff was one of the buttresses of the Faisan d'Or, he regarded with a high, if apprehensive, esteem. Even the mountains, the Persian saying goes, are afraid of a rich man.

Under the table was a tabouret for Monsieur's gouty foot. The scentless Dijon roses in a bowl were beaded with dew. In the crate burned a fire of pine cones. On the buffet stood the uncorked magnum of Chambertin, ruby-glowing, its soul expanding in the soft warmth of the room after the chill and long fatigue in the cellar. The air was filled with the etherealized bouquet of peaches and violets. Near the door a bottle of Rauenthaler, wired, resting on a shattered glacier, was as white as a polar bear.

And there was Pierre, of course. Pierre was the ugliest waiter at the Faisan d'Or, and the finest in all Paris. He was like a caricature by Daumier: squat, with bulging pale eyes, warts, and the bald, upthrust head of a toad. It was hypnotic to watch him conjure bread, butter, and silver out of the air, and he laid one under a spell as if a tincture of grace were in him. He was reverent before the food and wine. Like Paracelsus, he knew that "he who eats but a crust of bread is communicating in the elements of all the starry heavens."

No, there was no other waiter for M. Melun-Perret but Pierre, nor any other chef but Jules. They had ministered to him for twenty years.

The dinner was perfect. It was served late, for the guest had prepared for it first by hearing an opera. I helped Jules. We sent up the consommé. Then a baked pike à la Genoise.

After that a pair of *langoustes* from some Devonshire cove. Jules had boiled them; he cut up the meat, stirred it into thick *velouté* sauce with the pounded coral, a spoonful of meat extract, seasonings, chives, sherry, a half cupful of grated Parmesan, some sherry, and sliced truffle. It was the veritable black truffle with veinings of white. With this mixture he filled the shells, baked them a while in the oven, then coated them with buttered crumbs which he browned with a red-hot salamander.

Finally a Grand Marnier soufflé was put into the oven. Jules spoke for the first time.

"I am the guest of Monsieur tonight, and I beg you will do me the honor to dine with me."

Pierre, who had been scampering up and down the stairs, bowed us to a table set in a little arbor outside. He whipped the consommé to us; then, after the correct space, the pike and the *langouste*. Our courses synchronized with those upstairs. So did the wine-drinking; our part of the Chambertin and so forth coming down in a silver carafe. Pierre was in two places at once.

Jules had roasted the ptarmigans in a copper reverberator, shielding them the first half hour with vine leaves. The skin was like brown-glazed paper. There was bread sauce, a simple gravy, a dish of Flemish asparagus. Pierre carved, and served Monsieur upstairs and the gentlemen in the arbor.

He oozed in, rubbing his hands.

"He is charmed. And he begs you to pay particular attention to the second joint."

Pierre mixed the salad. The romaine and cress he doused with walnut oil chilled to an emulsion, turning it with wooden forks so that the bruises showed on the green in dark lines. He poured on the souring of wine vinegar and the juice of young grapes, seasoned with shallots, pepper and salt, a squeeze of anchovy, and a pinch of mustard. At the Faisan d'Or the salad was in wedlock with the roast.

Pierre himself ate only bread. He was an anchorite whilst serving distinguished foods. He ate large quantities of hard bread, with not a twinge of the cheek muscles to betray him, and only a minute twitch of the epiglottis to show it had gone down. But, unseen, he managed to engulf gills of brandy. He was a drunkard, and he was very drunk now, but only Jules guessed it, by the whiteness of Pierre's thumbnails as he gripped each plate. He came in with two quarter-pound truffles vaporous in snowy napkins.

"*Truffes sous la cendre!*" said Jules in mock surprise, leaning back in his chair. "*Fi donc, le coquin!*" he murmured as he put a glass to his lips.

"No?" asked Pierre.

"After the ptarmigan, no. Into the ash can with them."

"Exactly, Monsieur Jules."

I understood, of course. For a gourmand the truffles were permissible. Jules desired to cherish recollection of that ptarmigan. It had come from the moors of the cool Hebrides, where it had fat-

tened on gorse buds and myrtle shoots, its diurnal life a miracle because of the eagles wheeling overhead.

"Monsieur commends the soufflé. He sends you his compliments."

Jules declined the soufflé. I followed his example.

"Apples," said Jules, "and a piece of cheese."

Pierre looked at him with respect, and brought them. The apples
were Rembrandtesque, brown-red and flushed gold, for they were
the Orléans Reinette. My teeth crashed into one, as through flesh,
or sweet, crisp marrow, with an upsurge of cold, tangy ichor that,
like a blast on a horn, aroused heroic, ancestral memories.

"His first," whispered Jules. "His first Reinette!"

"This now, for the next bite," said Pierre, holding out to me a
sliver of cheese. It was Double Gloucester. "Alternate!"

Pierre must have been blind-drunk. I thought I heard him gig-
gle. "What would Madame la Baronne think if he didn't alternate
bites! *Hein?* She wouldn't give him another letter!"

My private affairs must have been discussed from scullery to
roof of the Faisan d'Or. A secret could no more be kept here than
in a nunnery. But I cared nothing, rejoicing to see in the basket
three more of the Orléans Reinettes. Coffee came. Later a motor-
car chugged away from the porte-cochere. Pierre rejoined us,
pulling off his jacket, collar, and tie.

"He'll be here in the autumn again. More ptarmigans."

"The dinner," said Jules, "was a success. M. Melun-Perret is admirable company."

Pierre tipped brandy into our glasses. His glass was a *bombe* that
held half a pint, and he sluiced it about, inhaling the odor with
closed eyes. We didn't want so much. After all, we had dined.

Pierre refilled his *bombe*, but his hands trembled in most perilous
fashion. He could not jeopardize that cognac, a Barbezieuc of 1815,
fully a liqueur. He wound a napkin about his left hand, which held
the glass, looped it about his neck, and pulled the other end down
with his right, hauling the Barbezieuc to his mouth in a series of
reverent jerks.

"*Salut!* A long life to M. Melun-Perret!"

We drank twice to the health of our patron.

"A remarkable man," I said to Jules. "You have dined with him often?"

"Indeed! Forty times, at least."

"What does he look like?"

"That I don't know. I never saw him. I have never had occasion, my dear young sir, to climb the stairs. Your health! And to the next ptarmigan!"

III

In Petit-Montrouge

I became a pupil in two academies. One was Beynac's atelier near St. Sulpice, where I studied modelling, the casting of bells and temples of Cybèle, with garlands and flights of doves, all executed in the best Demerara sugar. The other was Monsieur Paul's office with its wall of books.

There I plodded through *Grimaud de la Reyniére* and the *Almanach des Gourmands,* the *Roman Cuisine of Apicius,* and Traube on the *Gastronomy of the Ancient Greeks.* Monsieur Paul's copy of Dumas' cookery book was inscribed to Victor Hugo, then an exile in the Patmos of the Jerseys. A fat ledger in calf was the holograph work of the great Vitry, chef of the Rocher de Cancale—even more renowned in fiction, for there Balzac's Lucien de Rubempre supped with Coralie, and the ill-fated Rastignac dined alone.

My English I improved by reading the severe Mrs. Beeton's *Household Management,* the pages given to Sussex folk cookery soiled and dog's-eared. This British lady was less, I think, an artist than a social philosopher and moralist. She lauded a "Useful Soup for Benevolent Purposes" made of oxcheek and turnips. It affected me like a whiff of chill fog from the Thames. So did her discourse on suet pudding with the note:

"When there is a joint roasting, this suet pudding in a long shape may be boiled and cut into slices a few minutes before dinner is served, then browned in dripping.... Where there is a large family of children it is a most economical plan to serve up the pudding before the meat, as in this case the consumption of the latter article will be much smaller than it otherwise would be."

One can understand the incursion of British youth into Gaul, their haunted and anemic look—a flight from suet.

But the folklore was sound, and the steel-plate engravings of banquet dishes and the footnotes on turbot, or whatever else was "notably esteemed by the Romans," contributed to my learning. I am yet doubtful what learning is. You haven't it if you have just learned some fact or opinion, by ear, or by looking into a book. If, by sheer luck, you remember it five or ten years after, and can quote it, it is possible you may be indeed learned.

And in the kitchen I had Jules and Guido.

"Castor and Pollux," Monsieur Paul used to say of them proudly. He was accurate as well as poetic.

With the help of these twin stars he could outride any storm and tack the Faisan d'Or through any contingency: a banquet for a thousand World War medallists; a dinner for a society of Latin scholars who desired fare of the Antonines; a quiet repast for a Moslem envoy and his new little friend from the chorus of the Moulin Rouge.

Just as all sailing ships used to have their Russian Finn or Lapp, so all kitchens of the first grandeur have their Italian maestro. Even if they had not that monument to her, the Luxembourg, the French could not have forgotten Catherine de' Medici. Guido was from Venice. Venetians make good artists, spies, and historians; Casanova was all three. Guido knew all that was whispered in the Faisan d'Or. He knew about my letter from the Baroness, and knew the given names of Urbain's secret mistresses. Further, he was a geographer, and so learned in the arcana of foods that if you mentioned any point on this revolving globe he could tell you whatever it produced edible, and how much it was entitled to respect.

Still, he was pragmatic. I was with him at the soups these days. He kept ten separate cauldrons of stock on the range. He could tell each by the aroma of the steam it cast up. As he tended them he sang with tenor gusto and a lacerating throb: *"Zuppa! Ma che bella zuppa! Minestra e risi e bisi!"*

When orders came in, he capered from one pot to another, dipping his ladle into the stocks of chicken, beef, mutton, game, fish, turtle, and legumes. Ah, the furious swiftness of our Italian maestro, his flood of awful mediaeval profanity, oaths curling his lips, eyes shining with the gleam of a serpent's! He worked best after he had cursed and lashed himself into a rage. Never did he look into a book; he kept in his head the formulas of twice a hundred soups.

One day Pierre dashed in, eyes bulging out like doorknobs, thrust at him his toad-like head, and yammered: "Hang yourself now! It's the General Rossier. He wants Potage à la Bagration!"

Guido gave a snort. "That *cochon? No!*"

Pierre clasped his hands and wrung them supplicatingly, with a low cry of agony. A handsome tip was at stake, and the reputation of the Faisan d'Or.

"What brandy are they drinking tonight?" asked Guido.

"A Picquepoul, 1875," said Pierre.

"How good that must taste!" Guido patted his shoulder. "What would I not give for a tiny drop! Courage, Pierre! I'll see what I can do about that *potage!*"

Pierre scampered off.

The maestro's hands worked in a blur. He brought to a boil equal parts of *court-bouillon* and white consommé. In a little pan he sautéd a handful of chopped vegetables and sorrel with crayfish tails and bits of turbot. With four egg yolks he beat up a cupful of cream with a pinch of curry. At his nod I mixed all together, poured them into a silver tureen, and garnished it with croutons and a scattering of chervil just as Pierre returned with a glass of the Picquepoul.

"There you are, *crapaud!*" said Guido. "Your health!" He sipped the brandy. "Ha! My compliments to the General. Tell him to ask for a real *zuppa* next time."

As Pierre trod off as on a cloud, Guido winked and gave the brandy to me.

"After all, we should have some other reward than mere glory."

I gulped the Picquepoul, which blazed down to my toes and set them afire.

"Good?"

"Yes," I said.

He sipped a spoonful of hot coffee. Before a meal he never drank spirits, and my surmise was that tonight he was going out to dine, preferring, like most chefs, to dine elsewhere than in the scene of his labors. Usually he chose some small Italian café that nobody else had ever heard of. Give him a platter of entangled *maccheroni*, and he was blissful.

Guido was also adept in wares and delicacies, and the steward consulted with him before buying them in any quantity. He had also the key to the storeroom which ran the length of the cellar, its quasi-obscurity, as of a mausoleum—indeed, it had once quartered the coffins of priors, abbots, and a king or two—broken here and there by cobwebbed lamps.

He had a special room off this dungeon, redolent of mustard, truffles, jambons, gingerbread, and smoked meats and fish. From the beams hung strings of fig peckers, Corsican garlic, smoked plover, and wood fungus. An inky smell came from kegs of Czech-dried mushrooms. There were biscuits from England and certain hamlets in Brittany; boars' heads from Troyes, jellies from Rouen and Tasmania, *mortadelle* from Lyons; blocks of cheese, with more *chabichou*, or Poitiers goat cheese, than in any shop in the world; all manner of Russian, German, and Spanish delicacies, Madras chutneys, chocolates from Perugia and Genoa.

Guido was eclectic in his tastes. He could afford to be, so wide was his renown as a connoisseur of these viands "in the raw," as one might say. Dijon mustard he bowed to, but he best liked that from Orleans. His cockscombs he imported from Minorca, which breeds a finely crested variety of hen. They came brined in a vat. At the Faisan d'Or they were served in Sauce Éliogabale, a variant of the Financière, in puff paste.

Heliogabalus, by all accounts, was a nuisance in his day; and not much good of him can be said now, but his habits provided much talk, and he invented *vol-au-vent à la financière.* The learned Doctor Ellwanger believed fully in this claim. Chroniclers more skeptical think his cooks invented it, and that he killed them to assume their glory. The invention was startling enough to make him cut short his campaign in Syria and turn back for a triumphal entry into Rome. He passed through Palmyra on the way, in a chariot drawn by naked women, surrounded by courtesans, musickers, and buffoons, wearing the crown of the sun god, accompanied by historiographers to describe his genius and his orgies, and followed by his hundred cooks.

A trifle excessive, we might say. Still, if it was for the *vol-au-vent*—

Guido prided himself only on his skill with *maccheroni.* He had all manner of pastes in an alcove of this stronghold, sent to him from every corner of Italy. Rubbing his hands and smiling, he would nod at the packages with the air of a curator of State jewels.

"*Nous Italiens*—we have a paste culture, you understand? Just as the Mexicans have a corn culture, and the Cossacks and Mongols a horse culture."

For paste in its varied forms he had a delight. Here were little wafers, *fiori,* sea shells, cocked hats, butterflies, Cupid's bows, ribbons, wheels, ties, and confetti—the hollow kinds, the *tubini, canelloni, gnocchi;* the solid kinds, as large as a pencil, as fine as hair or moss, Genoese *orecchi,* or "priests' ears"; vermicelli that ran fifteen pounds to the mile.

Guido lived in a house near the Bastille, where he had a suite of three or four rooms. It was a kind of asylum for exiles—a dreary place, no more home-like than a museum, and his parlor, full of mirrors, horsehair couches, velvet portiers, and tall vases, all extremely ugly. He was hospitable, and often he had as many as five or six guests at a time. One night a week he cooked up a dinner for them in his kitchen, always some paste dish. If the oldest guest were a Sicilian, the dish would be served with almonds, chopped fennel, and sardines. If a Sardinian, it would be the tape-like *fettucine* with pine nuts, as Guido had cooked it at the Suora Nina near the Trevi

Palace. He was a sound judge of any endeavor in the field of paste, and loved the dish when it had the briny smack of anchovies or of the *vongola*, that tiny shellfish like a snail.

Connoisseurship exacts too often its penalty. Savors pall, the taste buds dull, the palate grows as indurated as the sole of an old boot or the conscience of a judge. Guido feared it. He judged the perfection of his soups by the twitch of his nose in the steam.

He was protected also by a childlike gift of wonder. This drew him nearly every night into some remote quarter, in quest of surprises. He knew all the *bistros* at Clichy where red-sashed navvies engulfed their ragouts. For months he made a pilgrimage to the Annamese colony in Grenelle, where he had surrendered himself to a beef-and-veal soup. It was tinctured with a few drops of *nuoc-man*, a briny exudation of decaying fish, mellowed for years in a jar.

One afternoon he waylaid me in the kitchen.

"Tonight you come with me. We shall dine. A paste!" His eyes rolled like a conspirator's, and his whisper was almost inaudible. "Not a word to anyone, you understand. We shall have with us— guess whom? M'sieu Melun-Perret!"

I think I was too stupefied to do more than nod, and gulp, "Where?"

"Chiusi's."

That evening, wearing our best clothes, we rode out in a bus to Petit-Montrouge. Even in spring and bright sunlight, that district is less than cheerful, but this night the squalor of the street into which we turned was heart-lowering. The air was like a cold poultice. The shops were hung with castoff hats, clothing, and boots, soggy in the drip from the eaves.

"Ah, but Chiusi's," murmured Guido, consoling himself. "Durum wheat paste, cooked *al dente*. And a buttery tomato sauce as they have in Calabria. I haven't been there in five months. We shall, therefore, approach it as a novelty.

"Melun-Perret? You see, he asked Pierre about it, and Pierre asked me. So I invited M'sieu to be my guest."

He was to meet us at this corner. In half an hour a limousine slid up, and Monsieur got out—a florid man, plump as a partridge, with velour hat raked over an ear. He wrung our hands.

"On!" he cried genially.

Guido was—what shall I say, apologetic? He deplored the district. Still, Chiusi's was worth the adventure. And its modesty in lurking in this purlieu of thieves, ragpickers, and slatterns was understandable. The mob, the tourists would never find it. It was no Faisan d'Or, certainly.

"I'd be sorry if it was," said M. Melun-Perret.

Blowsy, shrill women in rabbit-lined slippers waddled past, bottled beer and cabbages in their fat embrace. There were harlots, their eyes blobs of India ink on putty, their handbags moving like slow metronomes. Legless beggars shot by with a rattle of casters on the viscous pavement. The smells distressed Guido: the odor of leeks boiling, covered, in dank back kitchens; an empyreuma of rags and paper floating up through the gratings; the fetor of ratty, medieval centuries.

"There's a little shop here," said M. Melun-Perret gaily, "a little shop that sells ivories. I wonder—"

He lifted his hat once; he lifted it twice. He had been bowed to from doorways. He strode on happily, and took my arm, eyes alight, as mischievous as a gamin. He might have been one of the familiars of the Quarter, knowing every trull, pork butcher, and knothole in it. That rakish velour hat was a symbol: M. Melun-Perret was a Bohemian. He talked, he laughed, he jested. He sniffed before all the cook shops, appraised the snipe dangling in a café window, whistled, and twirled his stick.

Guido trailed after him, abashed at our flagrant conspicuousness. He was a snob: Petit-Montrouge was unworthy of Guido Tialelli, *cuisinier* at the Faisan d'Or.

We dove into Chiusi's. It was bare, with half a dozen tables; crepe paper in festoons dangling from the ceiling like concertinas. The only other client was a taxi driver partaking of soup, with a copy of *L'Intransigeant* propped before him on a cruet.

"*C'est un peu mortuaire,*" whispered Guido, as we sat to our table.

The waiter came out, a heavy man with vest unbuttoned. Guido read the menu. Baked Easter kid, ravioli, and a chestnut *polenta* were the offerings, and paste, naturally.

"Some of the kid, first."

"There is no kid. Nor any *polenta*. That is yesterday's card—and we had many customers. But I can offer you some spaghetti."

Guido held the card and his eyes drifted about him. Had he become aware that into this immaculate room, with shirred curtains on the window, an indifference had stolen like a faint miasma?

"The Signor Chiusi—?"

"Gone to Italy for a year. Family affairs, you understand—"

"The spaghetti, then," said Guido. "And first a little antipasto. A slice of *mortadelle*, if you have it. Some vermouth, dry. And soda."

"With the paste," said M. Melun-Perret, "a salad of cress would be good, and some young onions."

The man nodded. He brought us the appetizers and the vermouth. Then he pulled on his coat and hat and shuffled out. Guido peered into the kitchen.

"It's clean," he said.

We drank our vermouths. Time and again we clinked glasses. After the sixth clink, M. Melun-Perret blossomed forth as "Georges." A big yellow cat with eyes like rubies jumped upon his lap, purring like a sewing machine. He scratched it behind the ear and with the other hand combined more drinks.

The doorbell pinged, and the waiter slouched through to the kitchen, with a lumpy parcel, done up in newspaper, under his arm. The next moment he began chopping on a board.

Guido listened, with head inclined. The thumping was clumsy. He frowned. The flesh of bovines, ordered by nature as the link between us and the vegetable kingdom, should be treated with respectful skill. He leaned back in his chair and drank with eyes fixed on a calendar on the wall: a view of Lake Maggiore printed in indigo.

"The kitchen is *fairly* clean," he qualified.

" 'Fairly,' " said Georges, "is reassuring. You alarmed me at first. Never expect a perfect dinner to emerge from a clean kitchen. As well expect one from a laboratory. Revolting! A cook whose mind runs on soap and antiseptics is fit only for the guillotine."

Georges laved his palate with vermouth and smiled at us blandly.

"Now take Papa Andrieu at the Vieille Tour. His little kitchen is about four feet by ten. If its floor were trimmed with pick and shovel—which Heaven forbid!—the ceiling would be very much higher. It is an Alps of peelings, cinders, grease, impacted chicken bones, and bread. The debris of meals goes back to the days of the War—perhaps the Napoleonic Wars!

"Upon this he treads, this prince of Alpinistes, and what does he turn out? The most delicious of little Woodcocks à la Dumas; enchanting fricassees of eels; a squadron of the most disarming hors d'oeuvres. He climbs up and descends, like a lama in a trance, his soul absorbed in the confection of a Filet de Truite Saumonée, or a Bombe Valentinoise. The outer world does not exist for him. His eyes are filmed in meditation; his whiskertips drip gravy.

"Assuredly, where vision and the creative flame exist, a little honest dirt is no barrier to art. You go to a shop to buy a masterpiece that has taken your fancy—a Renoir, say, or a Van Gogh. Are you going to spurn them on the rumor, or even on the fact, that they came from ateliers that hadn't been scrubbed out since year before last?"

Guido echoed the full mirth of the great epicure, but his laugh was from the teeth outward. He ran a finger inside his collar and glanced at the clock, as if it were the face of destiny. There was no reason why that paste should be boiled to rags! He had been watching the clock hands tragically—ten minutes had elapsed.

Georges had shed his fastidiousness as well as his coat. Larger, more florid, and jovial he grew as he filled and refilled our tumblers with the rasping Algerian wine that tasted of rusty kettle. He was the raconteur born. He was as witty and amiable as if he were dining at the Quai d'Orsay with ambassadors. And right in the middle of a Pantagruelish anecdote of his village in Normany, the dish appeared.

Guido saw it first. Incredulity dilated his eyes; then he paled in despair, his throat contracting in a jerk. It was a pallid, glutinous mound, as gray as tripe, as ribbed as a washboard, and doused over with a pink sauce.

"It is long," he breathed, "long since I was here last."

He had fallen from grace, sunk in the lowest pool, reserved for the utterly damned. He had brought here, in his pride, the most renowned epicure in Europe, and amply had the gods punished him for his temerity. As the dish was set on the table, he flung me a glance—one glance before his eyes drooped—and his nerveless fingers brayed the crumbs on the tablecloth.

"Never," the glance said, "never let Jules hear of this!"

I think the cook also had caught that glance, for stupidity has not always the skin of a rhinoceros. He stood in the doorway, smoothing his apron, with an expression both defiant and furtive.

"And then, the mayor called upon Madame Goosefoot next," boomed Georges, filling up with talk what might have been an icy crevasse of silence.

We lifted our forks and began to divide the paste. Georges ate with gusto, alternating paste with salad and gobbets of hard bread. We had cheese next, then grapes and coffee. For another hour we lingered over cognac. Guido had revived. He was serene, even cheerful, as men can be who have received the *consolamentum* on the scaffold.

We departed. Before the tobacconist's, Guido slapped his pocket and gave a cry of annoyance.

"My pocketbook! One moment, I beg of you!"

He hurried back. Georges looked into the shop, then entered, and I sped back to Chiusi's and listened. The Avenging Angel had pulled down the shades. A voice bellowed with fear; there was a sound of fists crashing, like mallets on a side of beef. Chairs collapsed, and a table. A moment later the door was unlocked, and I walked on.

Guido rejoined us, and we stood under the street lamp. Our guest gave us each an oily Larranaga cigar. He held a wax vesta to them, and then lighted his own, holding it an inch or two away, puffing, until the flame shot forth and the tip ignited, winking in a halo of smoke.

I was conscious that his glance was elsewhere, resting on Guido's hand, bound in a kerchief, upon which a red glow was spreading.

We strolled as far as the Observatoire, where we shook hands with Georges. His cab whisked off into the fog. Guido leaned against the railing, head fallen, hat and collar masking his face.

"Let me fetch you a cab," I said.

"No." He sank to the coping, as if drunk. "*Ancora in cento anni!* Another such a dinner in a hundred years!" He lifted a hand to his eyes. "My young friend, do me a kindness."

"And that?"

"Leave me here. Good night."

My lodgings were three miles away. Being in the mood for solitude, I walked home.

IV

Monsieur Pom-Pom

The head of our art school, Louis Beynac was very famous, eccentric, and old—about eighty-six, I believe—a bent figure in a greenish-black coat with a ribbon in the lapel. For thirty years he had been struggling with an urge to retire to his vineyard in Alsace. But the desire to be useful to others was stronger. He took only those pupils who came weighted down with letters and credentials. He was just and extremely kind. I was entered at the request of Monsieur Paul, of whom he was fond.

At school I modeled columns, shells, flutings, and canopies—designs for *vol-au-vent* and Ducal wedding cakes. My notions of art swirled about classical ornament. Toward spring my sketches took the form of Freda Koepfli. She was like a tall sheaf of wheat. Her eyes had the velvety flush of an apricot. Her father was a confectioner in Geneva. He wanted her to learn design and later take charge of his cake factory. She lived with a maiden aunt in the Batignolles.

I used to walk home with her. Then, on Sundays, we would ride out to Versailles to visit the Petit Trianon, or to Sèvres to look at porcelain. Later we dropped all pretence of studying ornament and spent our time at the cafés, or in the country. She was the most beautiful girl I had ever seen, and I was in love with her. Therefore I had to see much of her Aunt Giulia, who, being Italian, had the strictest notions of propriety.

Guido made it easier for me by inviting us to his apartment for an evening of music, Chianti, and little batter cakes. And I would bring along a Siamese art student whom we all called "Pom-Pom," Manuel, the Colombian, and Rémy Ghismont, another student, who also was a culinary apprentice at the Faisan d'Or. His father owned a chain of luxury hotels all over Europe, from Sweden to Portugal.

There Giulia would placidly knit, listen to the music and the talk of the old editor, his wife, General Umberto Padaglione, and the rest of the group, so charming and so well-framed in the decayed elegance of the pension. I was part of it only by accident. But there I was, a friend of M. Guido Tialelli, and part of this respectable and old-worldly background, with its drawn portieres, horsehair upholstery, wax wreaths, dolmans, and the spinet-like piano with its ghostly tinkle and shaded candles.

Giulia, for all her austerity and jet beads, was youngish and plump. Her voice was musical. At the keyboard she would sing ballads of gondoliers and plaintive loves.

> Aime ton soleil, Italienne.
> C'est celui qui dort ton berçeau,
> C'est celui qui fleurit ton tombeau:
> Aime ton soleil, Italienne.

She became a favorite at the pension, and came to know almost everyone Freda and I knew at all well. By this time I was accepted as a suitor of her niece, though on probation. We had a very formal talk, sitting in her dreadful parlor.

"Your prospects?"

"I have a small income, a legacy. In two years I shall have a profession."

"H'm." Her eyes were as metallic as her needles. "Your relatives?"

"An uncle. At Vence. He has a factory."

"I expect to go to Nice for a week. I may visit him."

A tour of inspection. I shuddered. The prim Giulia, what would she think of my lusty uncle, the unbelted Dosso with his abattoir jests, and the alcoholic Baroness? I wrote to my uncle, after she was gone, begging him to be decorous for at least an hour, and to receive her in his best black coat.

How was I to know they were to surmise she was a timid little creature whose confidence would have to be won only by extreme geniality? They swooped down on her like an avalanche. They rushed her to the mountains in a big yellow tram which Dosso had engaged for the sake of spectacular effect. Under the delusion she was a gourmand, they dined her at the nougat factory, at Dosso's kitchen, at the hotel. In the same yellow tram, they careened through the lower Alps, Dosso in shirt sleeves roaring at the wheel, hunting for the prettiest picnic sites.

It was a month before Giulia returned, sunburned and plumper.

"How long did you stay at Vence?"

"Three weeks." She turned up her hands. "What could one do? That Dosso—*che numèro!*"

Despite that, I was approved.

Meanwhile, her niece and I were as good as engaged. I gave Freda a ring, an emerald set in a band of chased gold, which I bought for five thousand francs—all I had—at a jewelry shop near Beynac's. I borrowed enough for that night, from Pom-Pom, to take her to Foyot's for dinner and then to *Lucia di Lammermoor* at the Opéra.

To celebrate Giulia's return, the editor's wife decided to give a dinner at the pension, upstairs—a very simple affair for nine. The preparations got out of hand.

"The General will cook it," she had said. "He is a good amateur chef."

Said Guido in reproach: "Would you call in an amateur surgeon, however good?"

"This time you must be a guest."

"Madame," he replied firmly, "this is a case for professionals. And we must have surprises."

It was an evening when clients were few at the Faisan d'Or. Guido arrived early, bringing a fat Sicilian turkey and Jules with a hamper of London plaice—the fruits of their influence at the Halles. Guido cooked in the small kitchen, working fast, as if he had as many arms as Siva, and prepared every course but the last. Pom-Pom turned up in evening clothes with two jars of arrack. We took our seats, the General at one end of the table, Giulia at the other. Who, I wondered, was to serve?

Guido thwacked a bell. Who should dart in but Pierre! The good Pierre had come in to serve! He brought on the two-color soup, served bread and the dry amber Cortese. He dispensed pomp, as if he were the major-domo at the Farnese Palace. Suave he was, his porphyry-blue jaw thrust out, his linen gleaming, his hands never more dextrous. But he moved with a nimble and exaggerated caper, like a dancer in a ballet comedy.

"Mmm! *Quelle soupe!*" He sniffed. "Parmesan and nutmegs, eh? Whatever they have at the Faisan tonight, it's dishwater!"

Then came the whiting, fragrant of the North Sea, glazed in paper, which opened with a steam of anchovy sauce, one of Guido's subtleties, with a base of chicken stock. Conviviality and easy talk unfolded in the warm, perfumed air and the soft lights. The asparagus was fat and green, crisp with fried crumbs, giving way at the weight of the fork. Unobtrusive was the Tuscan myrtle wine poured with it.

Who could have divined what was in the *pièce montée?* It was a casket of puff paste with heraldic designs. Inside was the turkey, boned, roasted brown, with ox tongue inside, redolent of Madeira, and packed in truffles, chestnuts, and the celery-scented green lovage. Guido sliced it across with a knife like a yataghan, and the segments fell over, marbled and vaporous in their rings of pastry. The knife steamed, and he drew it delicately under Pierre's nose. Pierre inhaled with eyes closed. An appreciative tremor went through his frame.

"Melun-Perret, my poor one," he breathed, "you have never eaten!"

Guido shivered a little, as he poured on the Sicilian sauce.

"With this," declaimed Pierre, "the Grand Purple!"

He served the Montepulciano. The aroma of it—a mellow, winy tapestry, woven patiently by six decades of time in some dark Apennine crypt—filled the room. We were not alone. History, art, and religion crowded in with the music of trumpets and gnawing horns. General Padiglione murmured as if in a prayer. The purple reflecting against his thin, marmoreal face colored it like a portrait in a church window. He drank reverently, in the minutest of sips. Pierre, in the silence, inaudibly slid before each guest a salad of cress lightly tumbled in oil.

"Wine is made to drink!" shouted Guido. "Pour it down!"

Freda held out her glass to me, and we clinked. Her mouth had a stain as of mulberries.

The turkey was immense. Its year of life had been rendered blissful by a diet of pine nuts, milk, and locusts. The guests ate it with slow voracity and the serious, fixed eye of *gourmandise*. Though the wine spurred the tongue, the dish fostered that mood, far beyond gaiety, which touches the sensitive who contemplate perfection in any form, and are grateful and meditative. And these were guests of cultured palate.

Jules ate with bulging cheek, an admiring eye upon his colleague.

"Absolute! Do you hear that?"

"Tintoretto," said the General. "And Verdi. This is utmost fame!"

"He has," said Pom-Pom in his thin, crystalline voice, looking at him through horned spectacles, "too much delicacy to become famous in his lifetime."

Freda ate robustly, washing pastry, meat, and asparagus down her full Doric throat with draughts of Montepulciano. Her ring flashed in the candlelight. Pierre, fascinated by her appetite, hovered about her, with soft, encouraging whispers, slipping tidbits to her plate, furtively as if he were palming cards, with fork and spoon, which he manipulated with one hand in the style of tongs.

I wrenched myself away to the kitchen, for I had the dessert to make. Pierre followed me, and his voice was husky with admiration.

"There's a healthy one. *Elle a de l'estomac.*"

The peaches I had already got ready. They were Lord Palmerstons, early to ripen, and extremely good this season. *Pêches Giulia* I have made a few times since, in souvenir of a happy night ten years ago, but I have not been able to improve upon it. It is rich, but there are dinners that will be faulty if they have not a rich conclusion.

You split firm peaches and stone them. The centers you fill with this mixture: a little of the pulp, some macaroons, sugar, grated citron peel, and liqueur, and a dash of almond extract. Fit the halves together again, moisten with wine, whiten with castor sugar, and stay them in the oven until they glaze.

Give each of them a base of shortbread moistened with a few drops of red wine.

Now for the Zabaglione, its sauce, a fair dessert in itself. Since you have the peach, you will need but half a dessert portion. This is the formula for ten. (I made it ten, because there was Pierre.)

Fifteen egg yolks, fifteen half egg-shells of sherry, five tablespoonfuls of sugar. Warm the sherry very slightly, below steaming point, in a round-bottom saucepan. Beat yolk and sugar to a batter, flavor with a dash of rose, vanilla, almond extracts, and a pinch of grated fresh orange peel. Sink the sherry saucepan into a larger that contains boiling water, pour the batter into the wine, set over a fire, and beat. You keep beating until it thickens, lower the heat, and keep on until the Zabaglione expands into airy yellow velvet. (Remove at the right instant, or you are undone.) Spoon over the peaches, and hasten it to the table.

That was the dessert.

"Merci," said Giulia.

———

"A Russian I once knew also had a triumph with a dish," began Jules. "One great triumph. His name I have forgotten."

"Bulgakov," said Pierre. "Otto Bulgakov."

We lighted cigars and sipped the rice sake that Pom-Pom warmed for us at the spirit lamp. Freda, with elbows on the table, pillowed her chin in her hands to listen, and the emerald blinked into my eyes, which was her intention.

"Otto was chef to a Grand Duke, and accompanied him on a voyage to India. They journeyed to the interior, beyond the Deccan, and, after riding through leagues of swamps in howdahs, upon elephants with silver chains to their tusks—which the Indian Prince had sent to convey them—they reached the heart of the old Mogul Empire. The Grand Duke must have had some motive for his expedition. Science, perhaps; or diplomacy. The Prince, an independent ruler, had no very great love for the British. He preferred Slavs.

"They arrived. They stayed two months in the Mogul palace. It was large and mouldering, full of clocks, red plush, greyhounds, and shabby Bavarian furniture. The banyan trees about it were crowded with monkeys. The Grand Duke changed his uniform twice a day. There was banquet after banquet held in his honor; all the native rulers attended; there was much talk on science, or perhaps diplomacy. Otto was no Talleyrand. So he spent most of the time, when he wasn't fishing for carp, in the kitchen.

"The old chef was a phenomenon. He was ninety, wore a turban with a plume on it, and carried a saber. The last of a great line of Mogul chefs whose office was hereditary in this feudal domain. A civilized race, you understand, these Moguls. Cookery is a religion with them, higher than any other art.

"He drank water, this chef, and lived on nothing but corn wafers, baked for him by his own retainer. Anchorites have saved their souls on that diet. This old *gaillard* saved his taste buds. His masterpiece was a curry of goslings. It had ghee, coconut milk, green bananas, ginger, fifty condiments and herbs. The intelligence of a great artist played over all this intricacy, and gave it cohesion and a bewildering charm. It was fabulous. At the very scent of it, Otto felt crude; at the very first taste, he was caught up to Heaven.

"He had the temper of a warrior, this Mogul super-Carême. Woe to his assistants if they were clumsy! He whacked them with the flat of his German-silver saber. The backs of even his best chefs were scarred like an old saddle. To Otto he was immensely courteous, treated him with every consideration as an equal, and told all there was to know about this curry. He was in no jeopardy—Europe did not exist for him.

"The Grand Duke left, perhaps no wiser in science or diplomacy. Otto was the gainer by a set of the Moglai herbs that went into that gosling curry; for the old warrior had spent a whole evening in the garden with him, picking them. Thirty of them would have baffled any botanist, let alone any chef, in Europe.

"It was a triumphal return for Otto Bulgakov. He contrived that curry in Moscow, London, Monaco, and Sofia. The Société des Gastronomes awarded him the Cordon Bleu; the Worshipful Guild of Vintners, the gold medal; the Alleanza Epicurea, the sash and medal with two clasps.

"Few chefs had been so signally honored. Otto declined Escoffier's post at the Negresco, and prepared the curry for an assemblage of five Maharajahs and twenty leading epicures in Nice. It was a little short of perfection this time. Before the Société des Gastronomes he tried again to recoup. The master encountered more than failure this time. It was a debacle. Since the Grand Duke was angry, Otto had to resign his post. The unhappy man, after two years, had run out of herbs. He wrote to India, spoke with herbalists, consuls, and import merchants. He found no help. He plagued the curator of the Jardin des Plantes, who was helpless in the matter. Otto bought a garden and planted seeds, haunted drug shops and Indian restaurants.

"This was ruin. He had but one chance left. Borrowing money, he voyaged to India, and tracked overland to the principality. For three weeks at Agra he was detained by police, who took him for somebody bent on mischief. 'Bulgakov' was hardly the name for a traveler desirous of avoiding suspicion. Released, he found his way to the palace. A month too late, for the old man had been buried, and all his herbal knowledge with him.

"Consular authorities shipped him home. Things went from bad to worse. Urbain gave him a little work to do, but Bulgakov had neither sorcery nor spirits left. Later he washed dishes at the Café

Biard, and at nights he mooned about in herb shops, talking to himself. He was found one day, floating in the Seine. A man ruined by a dish."

Pom-Pom brought coffee to the women, who had retired to the music room, and drew the curtain so they would not be disturbed. In the kitchen the concierge's daughter washed the plates. Our room, as we sat before the window, looking at the fog, the cloud wrack, and the chimney pots, was a whirlpool of smoke. After a dinner of excellence, and the warm sake, the talk was mild and philosophical. To the chefs, closed in by their sedentary art, the world was a spectacle of which they could have but an intermittent glimpse. Not men, but growing things pleased them, and nature—rivers, cattle grazing knee-deep in herbage, birds in the park, the rows of opened crates of legumes, shallots, lettuce, and marrows before the shops in the shadow of St. Mathurin. Their eyes had been well-pleased. The orderly march of the seasons gratified them, and the affairs of men, whose quirks had irritated them in the kitchen, they could now consider bemused; they had slacked the bow for the night.

With Pierre, it was the reverse. He had been constrained to listen all day, repressed, to a hundred opinions, all at variance with his own. Today, for three hours, he had waited upon a deputy, a Bourse chairman, and a foreign minister, who had argued and banged the table from the hors d'oeuvres to the cognac. Unawares, they had been waited upon by a pent-up volcano.

It cracked now, with a hot lava flow of vituperation.

"Imbeciles! Swine! Conservatives!"

His porphyry jaw bulged out like a ram, bluer and more pugnaciously as the evening advanced. But Jules could always stave off a full eruption.

"A little of that arrack, Pierre." Or, "Mr. Pom-Pom will take a cigar, I think."

"Oh, pardon, pardon!"

———

It was school for me. Twenty such evenings made an academic course in philosophy; for here were two artists and an observer of behavior who, in the main, were wise, and content to play a subordinate part in life, and content with their callings. They talked well, and with shrewdness, for they talked about individuals. Who talks of men in general, talks of nobody. And there was Pom-Pom, with his chrysanthemum tumble of hair, goggles, childlike manner, and delicate sympathy, who was one of us, and a pet of the house. He was an anarchist. Only an unworldly soul could be so old-fashioned. He opposed everything on principle. Pom-Pom *contra mundum.* His ideas astonished and delighted everyone; his talk convinced no one.

"*E simpatico,*" General Padiglione, the old Royalist, used to say, in approval.

———

At midnight we took Freda and her aunt home in a taxicab. Then Pom-Pom and I struck out on foot into the mist, for I had decided to accompany him to his rooms in the deplorable Quarter of La Villette, behind the slaughterhouses. We prowled thus because we had not a franc between us this night, and with nobody about we could talk English as loudly as we wished.

Our Siamese had one talent requisite for the perfect gastronome—the gift of patient immobility. He was a connoisseur of rice. The hours we spent over various bowls of the grain in the Asiatic eating houses scattered in La Villette and the musty streets near the Sorbonne! We had pulao with shrimps at Banderji's, in Calcutta style; and Michigomi rice with tiny eels, knotted and baked in custard, at Mme. Kato's, where the poor Siamese students lived. Best of all, he liked the *kome,* which he cooked over the single flame in his room. Rice that he took from a withe-bound pail, washed six times, brought to a boil in its own weight of cold water, and simmered under cover for twenty minutes, holding a watch to his eyes. It emerged fluffy, dry, the grains separate. He ate it with a dash of *shoyu* sauce, or straight from the pot, as colorless as snow—and, to me, as tasteless. To me, rice plain is as utterly meaningless as one note touched on a keyboard. Perhaps an exquisite ear could resolve the note into many separate vibrations, exult in them all, and bind them in a unity. Pom-Pom could pitch twenty grains of rice, with a whir of chopsticks, into his mouth, then lay his chop-sticks down and blink in a grateful daze. Racial memories would flood his being: his childhood, the paddy-fields, the songs of his playmates, paper lanterns dangling in the mist. In the beginning was rice. He was a wanderer who had long ago severed his ties, through a passion for personal freedom. But, I fancied, he was not as completely cut off as he thought. A mouthful of rice, and the past was with him again, and he was close to the spiritual resources that may be tapped therein.

A man's best teachers often stand outside his field. From Pom-Pom I learned, apart from rice, much that was good. He was a *fin gourmet* because gastronomy, like every other art, made life vivid. And for the same reason he was a philosophical anarchist. Anarchists are not the worst company in the world. Pom-Pom carried not a bomb but a red sash about his middle, to proclaim his absence of political faith and to hold up his corduroys.

Outwardly, he was a Bohemian, in panoply of mane, velvet hat, and cloak. A few of the instructors at Beynac's were good speci-mens of this genus, as if Murger himself had designed them. He was desperately poor. When he sold a picture he was rich. In be-tween periods of such splendor he froze in his attic—a large one, though—and dined on a plate of rice and a nip of tea.

Pom-Pom had the aspect of a highly groomed little idol; he was a devoted slave to his friends, and he spoke perfect English, mixed with slang, for he had stayed three or four years in London, leaving it after he had got into trouble through his anti-militarism.

"Dammit, Jean-Marie," he said to me once, "I want to move out of my diggings, but I can't!"

This seemed hardly possible, for he was always moving, flitting like a bird from twig to twig.

"It's this way. There's a pair of bloody aristocrats staying with me. They're related to the husband of a second cousin of mine, who married a Japanese; and since they look upon me as a kind of rela-tive, they've moved in. One's a banker, and collects fourteenth-century maps and Arab sextants; the other is a tinned-crab and lacquer nabob, and madly buys stone angels. Tons of them, positively tons! I'm crowded out. We sleep on the floor. There isn't enough room to cook rice.

"They're millionaires, and they're turned Bohemian. When they're not buying things, they're at the cafés, looking happy-go-lucky and drinking with models. But we get along. On the basis of art. They have an unbounded, fanatic respect for it, I assure you!"

Pom-Pom's father, though a prince in a land where princes were thicker than temple bells, was one of the richest of men, so I learned from Freda. But Pom-Pom cared nothing for wealth. When landscapes didn't sell, he chipped tombstones, or helped as a clerk at the bookstalls along the Seine. Sometimes he marched with the Salvation Army band, playing a trumpet. Single-handed, he defied in London the Japanese Navy. It was a gunboat anchored out in the Thames; no visitors were permitted aboard, and none within fifty yards. Pom-Pom went out in a rowboat, with his trumpet and a cluster of balloons, and played a tune from *The Mikado*. All on deck took it in the nature of a compliment. The captain and officers beamed; all hands came to the rail and smiled. Then Pom-Pom let go his balloons, which rose, spread apart, and allowed a streamer to dangle down. It bore ideographs that read: "Fellow anarchists, hail! Down with all Governments!"

The little officers were galvanized. A bosun yelled an order that turned the crew rightabout-face. The streamer marred the air for an hour, drifted to the mast, and stuck there like a moth, until it was furiously hacked down and pitched into the waves, where it bobbed defiance until dusk.

This exploit, on top of others fully as undiplomatic, made it hot for him in certain quarters. His allowance was cut off, and Pom-Pom without regret shifted his milieu from London to Montparnasse.

V

The Duruy Mask

It was an August night. The roasting shields drummed with heat; the air was in layers of blue vapor, denser at the ranges where grease sputtered, fluids hissed and bubbled, and spilled foods carbonized in a blink of dark smoke. Five banquets were afoot, and there was the regular clientele to be served and, above all, to be kept patient. The chefs had been irascible all evening, but had now passed from excitement to a state resembling trance, the apprentices capering about them like extras in a ballet. Monsieur Paul weaved calmly through a delirium of pans, whisked trays, vapors and voices—turning a spoon here, jogging a casserole there, pushing back another to lower heat, dipping a finger into a mayonnaise, flicking a gout of Espagnol from a pot to his mouth.

"Look," said Rémy, driving an elbow into my ribs. "They've come!"

The brass-studded door had been thrown open.

"The Council of Brillat!"

There stood seven men in the formality of sash and rosette. Two would have been blinding enough—but seven! For an instant paralysis seized upon the chefs and their apprentices. It was as if among a band of monks at their devotions the Pope and six cardinals of eminence had suddenly appeared.

Urbain, waving to right and left with slow, grandiose movements, murmured the names of the chefs. Monsieur Paul, a cloud of gleaming starch, hurried over, confused and delighted, adjusting his kerchief and toque.

"The Council of Brillat," whispered Rémy. "And that's the president, Gaspard Duruy—the *grand cochon!*"

I peered through the steam. Who had not heard of Duruy—president of three gastronomic clubs, founder of the august Council of Brillat, wine taster and sybarite, editor of *Le Monde Culinaire?* He was dark-purple, breezily jovial, corpulent, with the jaws of a gorilla, and a monocle. Secretly he was a wine agent. He wrote a monthly *causerie*, after making the rounds of the five or six restaurants he favored with his patronage. Some of these, to the fury of their cellarmen, thus found it advisable to buy fluids of his recommendation, which they sold off at a loss to near-by cafés, or marked for use in the kitchens.

Urbain disliked and half feared him. He would have preferred to see in the Faisan d'Or a mob of Bashi-Bazouks than one Duruy.

But how widely Duruy was hated I never guessed until weeks later.

Rémy whispered the other names. The thin gentleman with face like alabaster was Monsieur di Valmonte, brain surgeon, violinist, author of a notable work, *La Cuisine Aphrodisiaque chez les Romains.* Then there was the swarthy Don Vicente Gonzalez of the Argentine Opera, wide at the cheekbones, known affectionately to the chefs as "El Indio."

(Don Vicente and I were to become the closest of friends, and I cherish his volume of memoirs, so honest that it was devoid of a single name in the theater or politics. He had several mistresses, whose noses were Grecian, who were never too young, and whose eye hollows were like volcanoes in quiescence.)

The advent of the Council was no surprise, after the first stir; the kitchen was prepared for the honor. Fresh linen had been distributed; the hanging rows of copper pots and cauldrons, like tympani, shone with the luster of gold. The seven men stood around, watching, smiling graciously. Monsieur Paul and di Valmonte were deep in converse. It was indeed an impressive occasion—the century dinner of Brillat-Savarin himself! The menu was a composition of Duruy's. It was tacked on the pillar near me, and I have written it down:

> Whitstable oysters
> Potage Crécy
> Carpe Miroir à la Chambord
> Truite garnie, sauce Genoise
> Caneton de Rouen en chemise
> Petits pois à la Française
> Artichauts à l'Escoffier
> Pommes rondantes
> Salade Marigny
> Bombe glacée
> Bonbonnière de petits fours

A modest dinner—but the Council cultivated simplicity at times!

Monsieur Paul called me over and introduced me to di Valmonte, who displayed to me a basket of shrimps nesting in frozen seaweed. Duruy, cigar in mouth, looked on with something between contempt and irritation.

"You perceive these?" asked the surgeon. "You recognize them?"

"Shrimps from Calabria," I said. "You are fortunate, M'sieu le Docteur."

"Cook them in a good peasant style," Monsieur Paul commanded. "A la Calabrese. Take them! *Dépêchez-vous!* Make a surprise for the doctor's colleagues."

How they would harmonize with the carp and the trouts I could not guess, nor imagine what the President would think.

I sped to my range. Shrimps I had cooked often on the *Piccolo*, and for better men than Duruy.

I heated oil and butter in a pan, browned a chopped bundle of green onions, a grated carrot, a small handful of parsley, and four cloves of garlic. Then I added five peeled tomatoes. These I cooked in enough bouillon to cover, and then poured in a pint of white wine. Then the condiments: a pinch of Spanish saffron, ground peppercorns, salt, some cayenne, and enough brown sugar to fill the palm.

I thickened the sauce with a dark *roux*, and poured in a glassful of sherry. After three minutes of ebullition, I forced it through a coarse sieve into a casserole. The shrimps, picked, went in. For twenty minutes they simmered, and at intervals I cast in a nut-sized lump of butter, a half cupful in all.

Upstairs they went, on silver plates, served on slices of bread fried in oil with a clove of garlic in it, and scattered over with chopped parsley.

Meanwhile I had vegetables and soups to dish out with Rémy's help, and pork chops to grill for my fellow apprentices' supper.

A clap on the shoulder. I turned.

"Superlative!" Pierre shouted above the roar of the kitchen. "I blazed it with cognac. They drank with it a Manzanillo. Duruy was in a rage!"

"Indeed?"

"His perfect dinner is ruined—and di Valmonte and El Indio took your shrimps twice!"

Next day I was summoned to the office. Standing with Monsieur Paul were Urbain, Pierre, Jules, Guido, and the linen man, from whose extended palms lifted a tall snowy funnel with a mushroom top—a chef's high bonnet, like Monsieur Paul's own.

Urbain read a letter from the Council of Brillat. Its couching was in terms most elaborately praiseful. And, among the seven names appended to it, was Gaspard Duruy's!

I broke into confusion and cold sweat, and Monsieur Paul fitted the bonnet upon my head. It was like being invested with a brevet, or with a degree at the Sorbonne. I, Gallois, had attained it in two years instead of the usual four. And when I returned to the kitchen,

I was greeted with a salvo as of artillery, the chefs pounding with iron spoons, and the Senegalese porter, a bottle in each fist, banged out a martial rhythm on a cauldron as if it were a tambour.

—

A month later Rémy, Freda, Pom-Pom, Manuel with his mistress, La Flamande, and I went after the night class at Beynac's to a Moroccan café, Chez Kashbah, for late dinner. The waiter brought me with the coffee an ink-damp *Excelsior*. My glance fell upon an item on Duruy: he had expired of a syncope whilst playing chess at the Café Harcourt.

I sat pondering, and watching Rémy and Freda dance.

She liked him. She liked his manners, his flattery, his knowledge of the world. He was half Swiss, and hotel was in the blood of the Ghismonts as it was in the Koepflis.

Rémy was handsome, two years older than I, and a spendthrift. His allowance he spent dissolutely in three nights. There was not an under-chef or a waiter at the Faisan d'Or who would not have hastened to be out of pocket for him, for they all dreamed of a high post in the Ghismont hotel chain. But Rémy never borrowed from these, nor from the chefs.

He had no disposition for the culinary life. But he had his talents: he could sing, he was a mimic. He mimed Monsieur Paul's paroxysms of wrath; the lip-smacking histrionics of Duruy tasting a sauce; Pierre hurling himself into the kitchen, bellowing in fury, his breath coming in the frothy gasps of a stuck ox. Rémy was an observer. *"Je connais ces gens-là!"* And how well he understood them!

Further, after Pom-Pom, he was the best modeller in our class at Beynac's. Those long, supple fingers of his were truly gifted with the clay. I was never more than fair, but we got the foundation, all of us, and Pom-Pom and Rémy above all.

When he escorted Freda back to the table, I told him of the passing of Duruy. We all bore up well under the calamity.

"Duruy," I remarked, "had taste."

My eulogy died there, for lack of more to add to it, but Rémy stared at me, his mind elsewhere.

"Listen! That game of piquet last night wiped me out, old chap. You have nothing either. Duruy can do a humane thing once in his life by earning us a stack of Napoleons.... Have you bus fare?"

"Twenty francs."

"That's enough."

"For what?"

"Who was Duruy? The leading gastronomer of Paris! Great enough, like a Coquelin, to be honored by a death mask! We'll make one of him—and sell it to the Alliance des Arts Culinaires for ten thousand francs. Cheap at the price, too. They can hang it in their lounging room."

Rémy glanced calmly at his watch. "We shall have to go, Jean-Marie, Pom-Pom, and I. Will you excuse me, Freda? And will you, my good Manuel, be so good as to call a taxicab and escort Freda home when she is ready? This is a matter of great importance to us, and we must be on our way."

That was Rémy—highhanded and selfish when his will was bent on accomplishing anything. I protested all the way to La Villette and up the stairs. Pom-Pom listened owlishly to Rémy's plans. He looked unmoved behind his thick glasses, but inwardly he was staggered.

"My dear Monsieur Ghismont," he murmured, "are there not certain formalities—?"

"Nonsense! Go to Beynac's, old chap, and bring back some plaster and clay. We'll wait here for you."

Pom-Pom gave me a helpless glance, but obeyed. When he returned, we drove to Duruy's house in the Rue de Bac. The concierge admitted us. In the salon was a notary who received us, then led in a large female in black, who was dabbing at her eyes under a mourning veil.

After Rémy made our proper condolences, he said, "Madame, we have been sent by the Alliance des Arts Culinaires, to make a mask of their honored ex-secretary. And if Madame will now be so kind as to grant us the privilege—"

Pom-Pom and I quailed before her outburst of hysteria. The notary soothed her, and spoke gently on our behalf: after all, a mask would gratify the members, and render a distinct service to future generations. . . . Madame glared at us in a damp and jealous fury.

"Ten minutes, then," she screamed. *"Allez!"*

Rémy bowed, and we followed him into the upper suite. I locked the door and sat in the antechamber, looking in through the door. Rémy and Pom-Pom built a clay dam about Duruy's head on its pillow, and then mixed up plaster in a washbowl. Then Pom-Pom joined me, and we lighted cigarettes.

Every few minutes Madame banged and screamed at the door, and was led off in another emotional fit.

Rémy called out jauntily, "Ten minutes, and the plaster will be set."

We could hear the crackle and swish of a newspaper as he fanned the mould to hasten its drying. It was taking longer than we had thought. Madame's hysteria increased; she rattled the door-knob, wailing. Even the notary began to thump. Rémy strolled into the antechamber.

"I forgot to oil the face. The mould has stuck, worse than glue."

He opened the casement and looked down into the garden. His hands were shaking, but his face was impassive. "Twelve feet. It won't hurt us if we land in the rosebushes."

He returned to the bed. For an eternity we heard him wrestling with the mask. Then he tottered in, pale and exhausted. "I can't! We'll have to run for it!"

"Try again," counseled Pom-Pom softly. "I'll keep talking through the door to quiet them. Hurry!"

We sat looking at each other in horror. Finally Rémy murmured, "His face will come off too."

Pom-Pom sped into the chamber. The uproar began again in the passage, and now came the banging of the notary's dry fist; he was impatient, for Madame was by now more than he could manage.

Rémy shut his eyes and inhaled deeply at his cigarette. We could hear the thumping of head on pillow in the bedroom—the furious fighting with an inert weight—Pom-Pom's breath coming in gasps. There was a loud *plop.* He shot backward, catapulted over the footboard. Then he bounded up, came to us, and showed the concavity of the mould.

"Perfect," he said gently.

Rémy collapsed, nerveless, as might a suit pushed off a nail. I threw open the door; Madame rushed like a tigress into the chamber; and the little notary helped me carry Rémy to the salon while Pom-Pom packed the mould into his bag.

"It was a great strain on our artist," I explained, and a painful task. But, then, Monsieur Duruy had so many devoted friends—"

"Indeed?" The notary, as if I had uttered some feeble joke, scanned me from the corner of his eye. Then, seeing our grave faces, "Indeed?" he remarked again. "I—I did not know."

I had occasion to remember his tone of surprise, of incredulity. I thought of it as we three rode back to the café. Kashbah brought us out some arrack, two quarts in all, enough to keep his establishment going a month, and we drank it up. That was a night.

A foundry at Javelle made a bronze cast of the mould, charging Rémy something like a hundred francs. It was thin, of skillful workmanship, and perhaps too life-like.

Rémy called upon officers of the gastronomic societies, but their eyebrows, as he spoke of Duruy, went up as if at some indelicate reference. The staff of *Le Monde Culinaire* regretted it had not ten thousand francs to spend on a memorial, not even two thousand. Rémy, a youth of sensibility, was shocked at this callous indifference.

"As well try to sell a bust of the prefect of police to the Apaches," Guido told him.

Rémy tramped from one club to another, making the round of the ultra cafés and vintners' conventions, his hopes and price sinking weekly. He dispatched Pom-Pom to call upon Madame. But after a glance at the mask she sent the concierge for the police, and fainted. The Council of Brillat alone was not approached, for it cared not to be reminded of its late incubus.

When the price dropped to a hundred francs, Rémy flung the gargoyle into a dusty broom closet. Broke again, he dragged it out and found that verdigris had given it a notable green patina. Some rag man, under the delusion that it was copper, might reimburse him with a handful of centimes.

But Pom-Pom had discovered on the Seine, near the bookstalls, a barge rigged up as a phrenology studio. Thither we hurried, and Rémy made a speech to the old Professor in skullcap; here was the last opportunity for the disciples of Lavater, the immortal founder of the science of bumps, to buy a genuine Inca head in bronze. He unwrapped the package.

"An Inca!" mused the Professor. He recoiled slightly as the head was exposed. *"Quel Inca!"*

"Un type digestif," said Rémy. "Very rare indeed. Even the Museum owns not one specimen of the gastronomical Inca."

"But two hundred francs!" quavered the old Professor, his fingers twitching, nevertheless.

"A hundred and eighty, then."

And so we left Gaspard Duruy in the canal barge and marched home, Pom-Pom playing a mouth organ, and Rémy between us, solvent.

VI

The Bishop's Arbor

"Here will be lilypads, and goldfish with tails like swatches of silk," said Freda. "And along the pool an arbor with chairs and tables. Like this."

She passed the sketch to me, and we admired it in the firelight as we sat in her Aunt Giulia's drawing room at the pension. She had drawn her self-portrait, a figure in the garden, dressed in a Provençal kirtle and shirred cap. All of us had suggestions for the tavern. Guido thought we should have a sign hanging from a post carved to resemble a dragon. Rémy preferred a big lantern visible from the Marseilles road below. These Freda sketched in.

On paper the tavern was complete.

It was all arranged now. After our marriage, we were to go on a honeymoon to the Tyrol, stay a while at Vence, and, after selling the share my father had left me in the nougat factory, leave for the Rhone to create our tavern. The Bishop's palace I first saw at the age of ten—a vision that grew more romantic with time. A green hill sheltered it from the mistral, which often sped with such force that lambs on the slope were blown away like chaff, and uplifted dogs trotted in the air, as if on an invisible treadmill. The palace had a round, ivied tower, garden, pool, and an olive orchard with a shrine, where "the old Bishop" had the resources of an admirable view, a spring, and the music of birds. It was bursting with legends. Fifty Bishops, at least, had lived there, but it was always "the old Bishop," as if time had made a composite of them all—those who had lived less than a century ago, and those who had lived when there were Popes in Avignon as well as in Rome.

Last August Rémy and I had bicycled down and visited it again, one blinding hot day, when the village shutters were closed against the glare. We pushed our machines up into the garden, where cypress and mimosa cast black shadows on the grass, and wavelets lipped with a cold tinkle on the edge of the pool. Frogs, like lumps of wet obsidian, swelled their chests on the parapet, and trumpeted to us as we unpacked our luncheon of hard bread, tangerines, and brandy. We had a bath, then a siesta. When it grew dark we talked, and from the Place in the village, where a regimental band was playing under a great clump of bamboos, music came up to us in spurts. We spent the night in the windowless salon, the Bishop's own chapel, where bats flitted and wasps had a nest on the ceiling with its indistinct fresco by Simone Martini.

Freda, who has seen the palace twice, was enraptured with it, and her father had written, proposing to assist us when we moved in.

"I am going to send Father this sketch," said Freda. "He will like this tavern sign."

"Much will have to be spent in repairs?" asked Aunt Giulia, looking up now from her knitting, the firelight gleaming in her shrewd eyes.

"Fourteen thousand francs, perhaps," I said.

Jules had introduced me to the mason who came to do some repairs in the kitchen. Jules also thought well of my dream. Most chefs at the Faisan d'Or had some such vision of an inn which they would own. But with them it most often took the shape of a half-timbered restaurant in town, with panellings, stags' heads, a royal name, and all the décor of spurious antiquity.

"If you would consent to come down, Jules, as partner, or head chef!"

"Not I, old fellow."

He had as good as quit the world. His life was entwined in the traditions and prestige of the Faisan d'Or. Its clients were his own. To serve them was he beholden, and among the ranges and stew-pans he dighted their meats with the bliss and devotion of Brother Lawrence, maintaining in the furnaces of his simple alchemy the spirit he carried as an acolyte serving at the altar. Is there wanting an analogy between him who sings Mass before the elements of bread and wine for God's purpose and him who prepares food "for a refectory table or any other table" in this world of ours?

Jules was the chef par excellence, a good man devoted to his calling. It was his one link with the outside world. To patrons who visited the kitchen, he was inclined to be brusque, or politely chill—at all events, he regarded them with disfavor. When they were up where they belonged, in the dining room, they were palates—a concept that was spiritual, and before which his attitude was one of self-abnegation.

Cognac, which he sipped down in the store room, was the only company he favored before dusk. Toward evening he glowed.

"Aha, here comes our good owl," Monsieur Paul would say, when Jules came up from the dungeon. "Something fancy tonight, Jules! Here's the list."

Jules had an atelier of his own—a corner smoke-blackened like a prehistoric lair. On his heat-sprung range the pots stood drunk-enly. Over his workbench a constellation of pans hung so low that he escaped bumping his head only because he moved in a furrow worn deep in the tiles.

Jules had that index of genius—productivity. In the same hour he could garnish crown roasts; turn out Mignonettes d'Agneau Maréchal, puddings Diplomate and Nesselrode, fillets of sole La Vallière, glaze à *vol-au-vent;* and perform alchemies with mortar and white-hot salamander. He was like one of those protean musi-cians who play on seven instruments at once.

All his dishes had the cachet of improvisations, and yet never veered from tradition, like the best of Sèvres, or of Chinese pot-tery, which is informed by the art-spirit even if it is but an endless repetition of the same design.

Pierre swooped upon us one night with a yowl. "It's the Maharajah again! And not a pike in the house! Ah, the—"

He came always without notice, this purple-black satrap with his dubious young friends, either for Scotch woodcock or a Mousse à la Belle Aurore.

"No pike!" Monsieur Paul went pale as curds, for the Maharajah was a favorite of Urbain's. "Then we'll use trouts."

"Monsieur!" said Jules quietly. He drew himself up, and folded his arms. "I beg of you to recollect that this is the Faisan d'Or. And for me, Jules, it must be pike or nothing!"

Monsieur Paul's jaw firmed. Then, after a few seconds, he inclined his head in a bow. The reproof was deserved. "Pardon," he murmured.

A chasseur was sent hotfoot to the Roi Nantois down the street, where he borrowed four pikes. We simmered these in *court-bouillon* and wine, pounded the meat to a paste, and built a wall with a backing of flavored rice. Jules poured in a *coulis* of crayfish, and in this fragrance swam diced lobster. He parted from it with regret. He stood watching as Pierre departed carrying high the silver dish, the *coulis* in blue flames.

"Only six have ever favored me with a demand for la Belle Aurore," he murmured.

"You'll make it at the Bishop's palace, with Freda and me," I said.

"Those Provençals, they eat only haricots! I'll stay right here!"

———

No, Jules was not to be budged. Guido and I were for going down at once to arrange the kitchen, scrape out the pool, and build hen coops. Rémy augured a casino, and a bar with an immense wine cave cut into the limestone of the hill. Freda was enchanted at the notion of croupiers and a cave, so well had the Ghismonts done with both in their fabulous hotels.

Here I see that I have recorded but Jules' triumphs. Let me recall now the shaking moment when grief was the portion of this excellent man. Pierre one night, walking heavy-footed, came bearing a salver and laid it on the bench. The Maharajah had rejected a dish of woodcock fillets à la Lucullus.

"*Pourquoi?*" faltered Jules.

Pierre could only echo: "Why?" He looked at me, lifted stricken hands, and withdrew as slowly as he had come.

I drew up two chairs, got an end of bread, some leaves of green salad, and Jules and I sat down to the dish. It was as hot as it was beautiful. It was perfect, almost. Wherein lay the flaw in the emerald, the false note in the madrigal, my critical faculty could not apprise me.

Jules rose and went into the garden, where he sat alone in darkness.

Alas, my poor friend! In time of heart-shaking stress, he was less a philosopher than an artist, and chagrin gnawed at his heart. I too, Gallois, have had my failures, but I have learned not to dwell upon them overmuch, but to fix my thoughts upon perfection.

Surely there had been no fault in Jules' technique. The *salpicon*—was it too bland? The wine in the *fumet*—was it of a sugary year? The crouton—should it have opposed the teeth with more crackle? Or was it merely that inspiration had failed the artist, and left his hand limp? Whatever the cause, the woodcock had been of inglorious flight, and fallen back into the covert. And in the garden sat Jules, staring into the silence, baffled and damned.

I do not regret telling of this disaster. When genius falls, it falls mightily.

Too often genius dares beyond its skill, or is overconfident. A reasonable amount of failure is salutary, for it reminds us that success is often but a truce between men and gods, between whom is unending warfare. The wisest of men will not deplore it overmuch. Success can no more exist without failures than can a bow without a string, or black without white, or heat without cold. Perhaps Destiny had done a kind thing in bedeviling Jules' dish. Fatigue lurks in the shadow of perfection, and nothing so surely dulls the spirit, whether of dictator or chef, as the monotony of triumphs.

Jules that night drank much brandy—four bottles.

A month later he could look back upon the failure without a twinge, and neither Monsieur Paul nor Urbain ever referred to that debacle of the woodcock.

The Maharajah, the purple-black satrap, gave us infinite trouble at times. Urbain liked him, and Pierre tolerated him because of the tips. Once the ruler had tried to secure the filigree salon for a peculiarly private little banquet, and was annoyed when Monsieur Melun-Perret refused to give it up on that night.

"I am dining alone," our favorite client snorted. "That blue-skinned savage! Throw him to the carps!"

The two patrons bowed stiffly to each other after that. True, they had never met, but each knew the other. It saddened Urbain, this gulf between his two friends.

"His Excellency's up there again," Pierre said one night. "He wants a curry of young ducks."

"He does, eh? *Le cochon!* If he wants that curry, very well then, he must give us his formula!" Jules said. "Let it be the patron's fault this time, not the chef's. I want that formula, and on paper!"

The Maharajah's curries were renowned. Their preparation was a family secret—hereditary, no doubt, like his throne and the jewels he wore at the Durbar. The Roi Nantois, our rival, had tried for years to get hold of that recipe, and was in dread lest the Faisan d'Or learn it, and serve that duck curry to the Prince of Monaco, and the Club des Cent and ensnare these clients forever—which was exactly what did happen!

Pierre trod upstairs. In a few minutes he came down with the Maharajah's secretary, a fragile, dark youth with a paper in his claw-like hands. He began reading. "Ducks—severed in handy portions. Now, fry lightly until set, and—"

He read in a curious, fluting, bird voice, and Jules set to work with a mighty clatter of pans.

"Again, M'sieu, I beg of you! A little more slowly," pleaded Jules.

The secretary obliged, then read to me. I looked for the apples and herbs. Jules began chopping up ducks, and I prepared the other ingredients. The secretary read and droned from the paper like a bailiff at court. He peered over our shoulders, and he blinked into the pots on the range. I could not so much as steal a glance at that recipe. Jules and I heard it piecemeal, and it was far too intricate to memorize. The Faisan d'Or would have paid five thousand francs for a copy of it.

We were in the thick of our task when Monsieur Paul came up, smiling and bowing to the ambassador from upstairs. We knew what he was after.

"It is execrable, Monsieur, that you should have to visit this den! Your pardon! May I—surely—you will, I hope—do me the honor?" He lifted a bottle of Madeira. "A little appetizer?"

The ambassador was measuredly amiable. They drank. They sat at the bench and drank again, and talked cookery. The kitchen was very hot, the Madeira was very cold, and the secretary was thirsty. He gesticulated much with his long, bony hands.

I connived with Monsieur Paul. The paper lay on the bench, and I read it as I passed by frequently, and each time memorized a few sentences which I jotted down on a paper behind the range.

The style is curious, but clear:

Sever two young ducks into parts, joint from joint. Cook them in three pints of boiling water. In butter make brown a very large onion, two apples, and three stalks of rhubarb. Cast upon this three tablespoonfuls of curry powder, and after all has cooked five minutes, throw into the stock, from which you have removed the fowl, and stew for twenty minutes.

Add thereto now a pint of chicken soup, and three tablespoonfuls of flour to thicken it and simmer another ten minutes. Sink back the fowl, and with it the milk of a cocoanut and a cupful of the grated meat; three cut-up ginger roots and some of their syrup; a tablespoon of British meat sauce. Brown slightly in a buttered pan a cut-up green pepper, which you will throw into the pot with three sliced-up very green bananas, a cut-up pimento, a half cupful of chutney, a teaspoonful of salt, two tablespoonfuls of juice of lemon, and two egg yolks beaten in two cupfuls of cream. Bring slowly to the boil, and serve within a moat of boiled rice.

The secretary went upstairs with his paper, unaware that he had been pillaged. When Pierre came down an hour later, his countenance was beatific. He shook hands silently with Jules, and then with Monsieur Paul.

It would be easy to prove that fine cookery has caused little infelicity, and still easier to show it has added much to the sum of mortal happiness. I memorized the recipe, thinking of my Bishop's palace, and then gave it to the Faisan d'Or. A theft, perhaps. But a sacrifice I had laid upon the altar of gastronomy. India could do no less to square itself for the fate it had dealt out to that unhappy Bulgakov, of herbal memory and a watery end. . . .

VII

CHEFS DINE ELSEWHERE

My uncle was accustomed to dine well at a tavern he often frequented near Hyères because of its quietness. It was an ancient tavern with Crusaders' heads cut into the stone above the door, but with nothing else to single it out above its rivals. He had to wait half an hour for a table. Motorcars and omnibuses were pulling up before it to disgorge patrons who had come for the roast lamb and apricot tarts. Its fame was resounding, though recent.

"Here, what does this mean?" he asked the proprietor over a glass of *marc* with him. "Have you a new cook?"

"The same one. But we painted his name on the sign. So now we are famous."

I am not metaphysician enough to explain this. Perhaps the cook had improved, to live up to the dignity of the signboard. Or perhaps everyone seeing it thought that here was the Napoleon of chefs, not to be missed on any account. But it is true that where chefs are anonymous *la gourmandise* in its transcendent aspect may not exist.

The Faisan d'Or was renowned not only because its food had merit but because its cooks were known by name and therefore praised. The names of at least ten of them were attached to a sauce, a garnish, a dessert, or a manner of preparing fish or a fowl. Be-

tween the salons and the kitchen were invisible wires kept at ten-
sion by couriers like Pierre and the major-domo. They would purr
that Blaise or Guido or Jules was in masterly vein at this moment;
or, in a voice pitched low in excitement, hint that Monsieur Paul
himself was this night turning out something special.

It was a subtle kind of flattery, also; the patrons felt that they
themselves had conspired in the making of a dish whose pattern
would never be exactly repeated. Then they would dispatch compliments, or even write off a note.

Guido received a note one night. He started as he read it, then
gave it to me. It was from Georges Melun-Perret, whose pleasure it
was that we dine simply with him on an evening a week hence.

"If he goes to the slums," said Guido, "I tell you it will be for
something good!"

The night came. Paris was dripping like a sponge. We crawled
through a fog that seemed an overflow of the Seine, trudged far beyond Notre Dame to the bleak, cobbled alleys of La Villette, and
fetched up at our rendezvous, a filthy little café on the banks of the
canal. It was noisy, full of tanners and abattoir workmen, all thirsty,
argumentative, and with pay money in their pockets. Dogs yelped
and fought underfoot, and were no more noticed than if they were
fleas. There was Monsieur Georges at a corner table, looking like a
drover in rough coat and mud-colored tie.

He greeted us and shouted for hot grogs. We were served by a
blue-jowled waiter in corduroys and visored cap.

"You did pick on a *sale trou* this time," said Guido. "You are also
a connoisseur in deadfalls."

Georges winked. "They know beef, these fellows around here.
The abattoirs are close by. Nobody knows beef so well as Louis
Jussien. A vast friend of mine from Normandy, bigger than five
slaughterers. He runs a coal-and-wood yard near by. He'll be here
at eight, after getting the meat."

He looked at his watch. "Past eight now."

"Well, this friend of yours, M'sieu Georges, I hope he finds it,"
said Guido. "But the shops are closed."

"Then he'll knock down a tram horse and carry it off."

A man of canorous voice moved toward us, arms outstretched— a giant in corduroys, unbelted, with kerchief around his neck.

"I couldn't shut up the yard until just now!"

Georges he greeted as one would a godchild, and we as if were cousins bursting with money and with news from home. He led us out, his laughter blasting a tunnel before us into the fog. To his apartment we climbed, above the fuel yard. How excellent it was, how sparely Norman! The chairs on the red-tiled floor were massive and thonged, the walls decoratively bare; against the window was a large table spread with checkered cloth. Here we sipped vermouth and looked into the well of the back street heaving with coils of fog.

"I was sitting here the other night," said Louis. "And under that lamp passed two oxen. Big as locomotives! I went to the abattoir in a great hurry. By good luck my cousin Guillaume was still there. They cut up prettily into fillets, I tell you."

"Indeed?" Melun-Perret drummed with his fingers. "We ought to have ten kilos of fillets for our club dinner at the Dauphine-Royale."

"Who will cook them?"

"Bosque, I think. Learned his craft at the Faisan d'Or and Foyot's."

"Bosque! Meat is not in his blood! His father, you see, was a locksmith."

Guido flung Louis a glance of admiration. This was an original, and worthily a friend of Melun-Perret, whose judgment was unerring. "But there are some, Monsieur, who think Bosque is good."

"They have not seen our fillets," said Louis. "Marie! The shrimps."

A *femme de ménage*, wide in the beam, brought him a bowl in which shrimps had been marinated in thick white sauce that was half veal bouillon. It was seasoned and chilled, flavored with garlic. The woman brought over a tray of condiments. He looked at it with one eye squinting at Melun-Perret.

"M'sieu Georges, if you can guess—you shall mix it."

"Shrimps à la Mirabeau," said Melun-Perret, pulling up his sleeves. "Permit me."

He rubbed a little beef extract in the juice of a lemon, added a handful of stoned black olives, some strips of anchovies, and threw these in. Next he added some torn-up watercress, mostly leaves.

"My weakness, but if you will allow me—" He thrust a knife tip into a pot of vinegarish mustard. Louis raised a hand in blessing at the alliance as Melun-Perret stirred all into perfect unity.

After we had shined our plates, "Why 'Mirabeau'?" boomed Louis. "Why the compliment?"

"In recognition of certain merits, no doubt," said Melun-Perret. "The arts can afford to be courteous. Look at *Sauce Diable.*"

Marie staggered over with a tray laden with four mastodonic kidneys, whose ruby meat winked in the matrix of fat. We had to poke and admire them. Louis himself slid them into the stove, to frizzle and snap like Chinese firecrackers.

"Valmonte," said Melun-Perret regretfully, laying a handful of cigars on the table. "My poor Duca di Valmonte! If only he was here now!"

"Two oxen offer but four kidneys," said Louis with reproach. "There is hardly enough for us!"

The haze from the meat baking in the oven was like an aroma made perceptible. The fifth glass of the amber wine was better than the first. More bottles were misting out on the window sill, and Louis drew in another. I felt that the evening, still young, was already memorable: the talk was good, the spirits convivial.

The recollection of any well-cooked dish fades if those at table with us were dull. You can be dull, like Brillat-Savarin, the worthy overfat barrister, and yet dine well—if you first take his precaution of inviting only agreeable and witty dining partners.

With an eye on the clock, Louis retreated to the oven. He showed us the kidneys with unaffected pride. They were crackled like old porcelain, roasted to the core. He sliced them the breadth of a finger, and glacéed them a minute under the flame. We took out slices from the hot wood, ate them with a powdering of salt. How they snapped!

The woman brought us hot bread in a cloth and wedges of cold tomato. No meal could have been simpler. Invigorated as by a tide, we felt a renewal of bodily and spiritual strength. Melun-Perret ate in a slow trance. The texture of the lean alternated on his palate with the waxy crispness of the fat. The slices disappeared. None was left.

"Messieurs?" said Louis, pointing to the liquor on the still hot plank. Guido and I shook our heads. With a crust, Louis dabbed piously at a blot on the plank. It was deeper than a blot. The bread sopped abundantly in a hollow, and he gave it to Melun-Perret, who feebly simulated protest.

"That hollow," said Louis, "my father scraped it out with the edge of a coin. He was a farmer and knew honest beef. It is—what shall I say?—his monument."

He made coffee over the blaze, and carried it to the table in a blackened pot. Meanwhile we had cognac from a squat bottle. It was robust and old, the dowry of a grandmother in Angoulême. It spread lambently over tone, palate, and throat with the light of shaken-out tinfoil.

Louis filled our thick, white cups with his brew.

"In my yard is a wood sawyer who is rich. He owns a leak in the engine. Under it he keeps a coffee filter. Every ten minutes— pouf!—goes a pinch of steam. At noon his reward is a finer cup than we can drink."

We sat longer over the coffee than over the meal. It was screaming hot, tar-black, and aromatic. Melun-Perret bowed over it with eyes closed, inhaling, his cigar rolled beatifically in his mouth. The baked *rognon* and the coffee had thrown him into silence. Man's propensity to praise, so often foolish, departs him when he meets with the highest excellence. One accepts with decent and quiet joyfulness a finer sunset than ordinary, a Molière play, a dinner of extreme merit. In aftertime to sharpen our recollection, we speak of them in praise.

The woman left. Louis brewed another potful of coffee. I drank mine simple and black. Guido spooned in plenty of sugar. Louis laced his with cognac, and Melun-Perret poured his coffee over a twist of tangerine peel. Where no coffee is, says the Arab, there is no merry company.

———

"We shall get the Doctor di Valmonte one of those fillets," said Guido finally. "He will insist on eating it with a pinch of salt, though."

"Still," said Melun-Perret, pensively, "no man has a palate more delicate, nor more curious." He lighted a cigar. The woolly smoke of it matched the fog at the window. One eyelid drooped—a sign that the raconteur was finding his vein.

"Di Valmonte, when I first knew him, was living on the Grand Canal in Venice. At his *palazzo* he pursued the art of dining well. It was an art he carried as far as it could go. He was even more devoted to his friends: a failing, perhaps, but it was his heart that was at fault.

"So his dinners were epochal. Figure to yourselves my trepidation when I was invited there one night, three weeks beforehand. I set out with three acquaintances, and we poled up the Grand Canal through a fog thicker than sheep's wool. The palace was very old, rearing five stories high out of the mud in which it had been planted at the time of the first Doges. A little ruined, and very damp, but incurably noble.

"A porter with a hurricane lamp awaited us on the landing. He had a mourning band on his arm, I remember, and the grandeur of a three-cornered hat. After all, the guests were members of the Royal Gastronomic Society. He escorted us up one flight of stairs after another. Up we went, winding on the spiral staircase, as if we were in an etching by Piranesi. There were statues, and ancient tapestries, and murals eaten by damp so that they hung flickering in the wind, like pennants.

"The upper floor was stately, thronged with persons of dignity and manner. Our cloaks were removed. An aged servant, who might have been a Cardinal in disguise, brought me an *apéritif* of Manzanilla. I was conscious that his hand trembled ever so slightly, that a blue shadow underlaid a pallor about his eyes.

"So I was not surprised when I began to hear around me the

murmur of condolences. Madama, Valmonte's grand-aunt, had fallen lifeless on the stairway six days before. Valmonte, though he had been no favorite of hers, decorously withdrew himself from society and his pet restaurants. The dinner, however, could not be postponed. *Noblesse oblige!*

"We moved on the *sala,* heads bowed, as if in a cortege. There a table awaited us.

"It was of subdued magnificence, covered with gold-embroidered cloth, roofed with tapestry like a catafalque, and set with tapers in heavy silver holders. The salads were frosted plants, basils, and great mandrakes, their branches hung with anchovies, pickled limpets, and snails, quail eggs, olives, cockscombs, tidbits of crawfish and lobster, olives and tiny vegetables—a yield glistening after a rain of caviar dressing.

"Then came mullets, roasted larks, truffles, and artichokes. Through them all interwove the rubric of signorial wines. But I shall not weary you with the details of a banquet that went far beyond the vulgarity of mere perfection. The meat was so worthy that all that went before was but a prelude. It was fillet à la Chateaubriand.

"It baffled me. My dining partners, Duruy on one hand, and Monsieur Gilbert Emery, the actor, on the other, at first were half agreed it was Charolais beef. Then we were less sure. I thought it was beef from the Tuscan marshes, where the oxen graze on fern. 'Zebra, perhaps?' whispered the actor, who had dined here before.

"Zebra is, on the whole, sweet. So we kept on with our riddle, venturing this, rejecting that. No gastronome in Italy could out-guess Valmonte in his whimsical moments. He had served ibis from the Nile, bear from the Urals, suckling boar from the Pyrenees, musk ox from wherever musk ox comes.

"The man on the right laid down his fork. Inspiration lighted his face.

" 'I shouldn't be surprised,' he whispered, 'if it were a joint off the old Duchess.' "

———

Louis was asleep. He had stacked pyramids of wood all day, and been a mighty host all night. We left, and strolled to Les Halles to see the vegetables come in. Tarpaulin-covered drays were moving past like elephants. The horses at the troughs lifted their heads with a jerk under the lamps. The water dripped from their muzzles in shining arcs, like scimitars. Dawn was on the way, and we hovered about, coat collars up, until five, for a breakfast of hot soup with the draymen.

VIII

Manuel, the Inca

For months I had been growing aware that Freda, though always gracious, was becoming less responsive to my attentions. All this summer she had found excuses for not coming with me on a picnic to Sèvres or to Versailles, and she had even declined an invitation to the Midinettes' Ball. Rémy had left Paris to work and learn the hotel business under his father. "I shall have to work myself up," he wrote me, "and I've started at the smallest Ghismont hotel, and on the smallest Alp, which makes it the bottom of the ladder." He had been gone since August, and it was now already November.

I knew that he was in love with Freda, but I was unwilling to retire as a rival. I wrote and wrote notes to Freda, and she agreed to come out with me, not to dance, not to see a play, but merely to talk with me for an evening. Her aunt, when I came to the apartment, was as chill as one of her Swiss glaciers. I saw by her rigidity and silence that she disapproved of my taking Freda out. But we two went, and sped on to Chez Kashbah, an old haunt of ours, both of us sitting wordless in the cab.

The old Moroccan brought us little drinks. He waited upon us with solicitude. He appeared to feel there was something wrong. Once he enquired if we had heard from Rémy, and that helped matters not at all. Then he wound up a gramophone with a lily horn, slipped in a cracked disc, as if hoping that the music of drums and flutes, wildly martial, as of some savage tribe in the desert, would impel us to dance. Then a knife fight broke out in a booth, and gendarmes dashed in to haul out two natives, locked in a deadly embrace, and heaved them into the police wagon. The "salad basket," as it was called in our slang, was not an infrequent caller at Kashbah's.

"A pity," I said to Freda, "but it was only a little debate. Now that it's quiet, you wouldn't really like a dance?"

"Not really," she said with calmness. "I told you before that I had no intention of dancing."

"Of talking, then?"

She talked briefly. "I had hoped you would have seen by now that my feelings have changed, Jean-Marie. I plan soon to be married to Rémy."

"I should have known," I said wretchedly. "But I never dreamed that you felt so warmly to him. I am sure it was my fault."

"No, Jean-Marie, it was no one's fault. It was I who changed, and when Rémy asked me to marry him I agreed. That was on the very day he left. And I shall be going to Switzerland tomorrow."

She wept a little, and tugged at the ring I had given her, but it remained on, tightly. I urged her to keep it as a little memento of old friendship. We both of us fell silent. Then I went out, whistled for a cab, and took her home. On the doorstep she gave me her cheek to kiss. I walked on to my flat, dazed. If a player happens to be under the curtain when it tumbles, he is liable to be stunned.

———

It was a melancholy autumn for me; so many of my friends were gone. Pom-Pom, the little Siamese, vowing he was in quest of the Nordic Absolute, went to live in Sweden and paint fjords. Guido went to America, to Long Island, where a cousin had bought a small estate and a mansion for him, and they were going to convert into a fashionable tavern. He begged me to come along, but I declined. If I had to be sad anywhere, I preferred to be sad in Paris. And I had just received a card announcing Freda's marriage.

"That's too bad, old fellow," said Guido. "I feel sure she was in love with you. And this is an impersonal matter, I dare say. A merger of the Koepfli and Ghismont interests."

"That's brutal!" I protested.

"It is," assented Guido. "So is life. Your health, Jean-Marie! And promise me you will come to Long Island and join me if life tires any further in Paris."

It was weeks before I recovered my spirits. Paris seemed empty; the world seemed empty. Gone were Freda, Rémy, Pom-Pom, and the dream of the Bishop's palace down the Rhone, with the sign-board rocking in the breeze and bees swarming about the hives in the garden.

Then Manuel, the Colombian, came back on a brief visit. He was the only one of my old fellow students at Beynac's in Paris this autumn.

I think he missed the old Beynac crowd as much as I did, and nightly he waited for me at the Faisan d'Or, to walk in the park, or to sit at the Café Select, and drink coffee.

Rémy used to insist that Manuel, when he first came to Paris, wore a blanket and a feather headdress—an exaggeration with a germ of truth, for he was as remote as an Inca priest, taciturn and haughty. His relatives, more than half Indian and ambitious, still kept him under their thumb.

We emancipated our Colombian. We put him through the ropes, took him along with us to the cafés, the music halls, the theaters, and urged him on the upward path. He drank pots of black coffee instead of pots of noxious sweet chocolate. With us as guests, he dined sensibly at the Dauphine-Royale or Noel-Peters.

A great change was wrought in him inwardly. He became a bal-let maniac. As a *flaneur* he surpassed all of us. He kept a mistress—a large blonde Flemish girl hung with jewels. He was familiar at the Café Select, where he dined with La Flamande almost nightly. The waiter brought him always the same coffee filter—a silver one with "M" carved upon it.

Then he returned home to his family and his cattle. He went under duress, and with heartbreak. La Flamande wept and raged, despite the handsome gift he settled upon her; she was genuinely fond of him, poor thing. She also had virtue, and proved it by returning sensibly to her husband in Brussels.

Manuel wrote me now and then. He found he had gone home too much changed, like all the young, part-Indian bloods in the somber capital of Bogotá, atop the Andes. There were many like him on that roof of the world, who desperately kept up a semblance of the life they had known in Paris. They dined at some deplorable table d'hôte, wore cloaks and opera hats, and drove to the theater, where a cowboy film was unveiled to bad music in the pit.

"Some of them fly airplanes," he told me, "to race with the condor and find a little more sun and warmth. *Los pobres!* They are exiles; their lives are bleak. Over the Andes the air is thin, the wind eternally howls and screams like a thief in flight. And often the planes crash on the crags. A few take wives. Some join the penitential orders, and with cowl and candle file through the dark rifts of the town, the clangor of the immense bells gnawing at their sad hearts."

So Manuel was glad to be here tonight. He sat formal and heavy, wearing an ill-cut German suit, yellow shoes, and a violet tie, more taciturn and more Indian than ever. Our reform work on him had gone for naught. *"Mon cher* Manuel, how long will you stay with us this time?"

"Two weeks."

"Absurd!"

He was not to be budged. He had to return to his cattle ranch atop the Andes, and had come only on business.

"To Bogotá?" I asked.

"I never go there." He shrugged. "I go to no city after Paris."

"You are married, perhaps?"

He looked at me stonily from under his hooded eyes. The ash grew longer on his cigar; it fell upon his waistcoat.

"Does one love twice?"

He puffed slowly. "I live on my *estancia*, alone save for a few gauchos. Often I ride away by myself, when thoughts are too much with me. I make camp in the solitude, and remain for the night before a fire. Then, in a silver filter that a waiter in a certain Paris café got for me, with an 'M' on it, I brew coffee. The aroma of it! The solace of it! I am elsewhere, and no longer alone. You understand, perhaps?"

———

A shift in surroundings has a healing value. I moved, with the help of the strong-armed Manuel, to a lodging house in a side street off the Bastille. Though dank, and its plaster stained with the rain in great splotches running through the chromatic scale of wines, the apartment was agreeable. It was a long chamber with spikes driven into the wall for clothes pegs, a washbasin, and a few splinters of furniture. The windows, which had looked down upon three centuries of history, gave out upon beech trees and a kiosk bright with magazines. There was no concierge, no surly warden at the entrance to spy one's coming and going and to hold up letters until a *douceur* was paid out. You went straight up the stairs from an archway next to a tobacconist's, where you paid the rental monthly.

Manuel put on old clothes and busied himself in painting the walls and ceiling with tumultuous set pieces—scenes from the Revolution; copies of Watteau and Fragonard; Andean landscapes full of volcanoes, charging bulls, condors; and no less than five portraits of Simon Bolivar at dramatic moments of his career—leading battles, signing charters, holding up the sky with his sword. Manuel hung a sheet of canvas from the ceiling, dividing the room to make it a suite, and this partition he embellished with nudes and divinities frolicking amid billowing clouds. I got in more furniture, and Manuel cut holes in the partition to receive the bureau and trunk, so that they should not bulge into the room. We had a little housewarming, and next day Manuel, refreshed by his immersion in art, left for his ancestral home in Colombia.

Beynac's, this fall, died the death, and was torn down to make way for a cinema palace—a testimony to the falsity of progress—and with it fell the old rookery adjoining, where so many of the day students had lodged. Dismay seized us when we first heard rumors of its impending destruction. It was like pulling down the Panthéon, or the Gobelins, or even worse than that, for this was a disaster that involved our affections. The master himself was the last to depart. Defiant to the end, Beynac stayed in his office, armed with a sword cane, and he stayed there until the door was pulled off the hinges and the stairway was ripped out with a cable attached to a truck. It collapsed with a roar and an eruption of plaster and the dust of three centuries.

Then Beynac appeared at the window, lifted his hand, and made a speech. It was a very touching speech, and his thin voice, firmed by indignation, carried through the clattering of a heavy rainstorm. He deplored the savagery of modern life that was so callous to the beauty of the past. He urged us all—students, gendarmes, newsboys, and carpenters, all looking up at him—to consider what our ancestors had done, and to refresh our souls in the grace and wonder of the masterpieces of the ages long past.

"I have fought half a century to preserve this building for you. The Old Guard has not surrendered. It dies."

A ladder was run up for him. He climbed out and descended, a roll of canvas under his arm, the rain sluicing upon his mackintosh and his thistle-white head. Manuel and I helped him down the ladder, and packed him off to a café-restaurant in the Bois. He recovered his spirits, was resigned, even gay, and over dinner and cigars told us it was Fate that had intervened, and was pushing him out to his cottage down the Seine, where he could raise hollyhocks and fish to his heart's content for trout. I don't suppose the thought occurred to him that of all the thousands of pupils he had taught, but two were with him at the end—an obscure *sous-chef,* and a stone-faced Indian from Colombia. Nor did it ever occur to him, I am sure, that these two pupils felt themselves immeasurably in debt to him.

———

Memories clustered thickly about Beynac's for us. Rémy's quarters were on the floor above the art school, and it was there that we once had an unexpected banquet. Improvident, but generous, Rémy often invited friends to dinner, even if his pocket and larder were empty.

On this curious night, fifteen of us had impulsively been asked in. Most of the guests, for it was the end of the month, were flat; fortunately, some of us, and the most experienced, brought along loaves of bread and some *jus de parapluie,* cheap claret. Rémy, after borrowing a hundred francs from me, behind the door, left to buy viands from the Italian cook shop three streets away. A caterer's van pulled up before Beynac's. And amidst the uproar outside—for it was the evening of election day—porters shuffled up the stairs, staggering, bent under the weight of trays. That van was a cornucopia on wheels. It sent up roasts of beef, turkeys, geese, vegetables, salads, ices, wine, and soup. Turtle soup, in huge tureens! The waiters spread the table, served turtle soup at once, and poured out Madeira.

"A banquet!" shouted Manuel, made articulate for once. He lifted his glass. "We'll make a start. To Rémy, good old Rémy!"

If the ceiling had not been so thick, the uproarious toast would have been heard by the Conservatives and their President, the newly elected Deputy LaPlanche, who were downstairs. La-Planche would have been deeply interested in the food, for he was one of the most particular habitués of Noel-Peters and the Faisan d'Or. Never had such a banquet been spread in this rookery, nor any devoured with such voracity. There was enough for twenty-five. The waiter sliced off only the breasts of poultry, and poured the oldest wine first. He worked dextrously, for he was a good waiter before the Lord and excelled himself for the glory of the house that had sent him.

A hundred dollars' worth of food and champagne had been downed when the door opened. There stood Rémy with a demi-john of claret, some bread, and a paper of sausage and potato chips. He stood fascinated. His mouth opened with the fear-struck expression of one gazing upon a miracle. The waiter was bent gravely over a dish, pouring flaming sauce upon a goose-liver for Pom-Pom, who counted himself lucky if he could eat a sausage once a week. Rémy lifted an arm rigidly. He pointed to the table.

"What is this? Where did it come from?"

Manuel, his cheeks bursting with goose and baked orange, just goggled fatuously.

"Who sent this up?" insisted Rémy.

Then everybody knew something was wrong.

"Aren't you gentlemen the Conservatives?" asked the waiter, paling.

"Conservatives!" yelled Rémy. "Not here! We are Royalists, with a jack-Communist or two, and an Indian—but Conservatives—never! Not on this floor!"

The waiter lifted hands to his hair slowly, then pulled. He bellowed. He went lunatic. He was unable to grasp the simple explanation of the mistake. The new Deputy had ordered the dinner to be sent in after a conference at the club, downstairs, because the upstairs room was being painted. And the porters, seeing a party of gentlemen upstairs in a high state of expectancy, had made a quite natural error.

It was a painful matter to explain this to the waiter. He grew violent. For a minute or two it seemed doubtful if anybody in the room could escape alive. The waiter was one of those who prefer death to dishonor. He fled, to yell for gendarmes and Deputy La-Planche, who would be certain to arrive outraged, and possibly go insane. As for the guests, the window offered the quickest way out. We took it.

IX

MAYOR IN THE ATTIC

I grew to like this Quarter well; it was small, provincial, as self-content as only a regional Quarter in Paris can be. The pork butcher, who locked up at seven to devote himself to his clarinet, introduced me to the other shopkeepers, the women at the news kiosk, and the café that was the haunt of my fellow tenants. This was our club. Here we met at night to consider the day's crop of happenings. Gustav, the Samson-like barber with the fan-shaped beard, had again to the glory of our Quarter won the hair-curling contest at the Batignolles fair. The tobacconist's kitten, treed up in the elm near the kiosk, still spurned the allurements of liver and a saucer of milk. An old mastiff, after a lifetime of neglect, had chosen to expire under the wheels of a grocery truck. Should Monsieur Justine, its owner, now loud with grief, press for monetary damages, or settle for a box of tinned meats and a little sound wine?

After the mishaps to fauna, politics was the great topic at our club. The Mayor, a rosy, large-paunched man with a thumbnail of beard and thick glasses, presided at the Wednesday night gatherings, which were an institution. M. Lambert was not rightly a mayor; the title was merely a tribute to his prestige and learning. He dwelt in the large room adjoining mine, at the end of the corridor. He lived on a tiny income that just kept him alive and sheltered. A relative, a farmer near Aurillac, sent him a fine Cantal cheese once a month, for, apart from being a philosopher, M. Lambert was a connoisseur of cheese.

All day he sat at his window, rotund and placid, looking at the pageant of life in the streets, the trees, the children at play, the shiny green busses rolling off to the country which he had not visited in thirty years. He scratched notes, read in large books, and wrote grocery catalogues for firms like Felix Potin.

The world being what it is, logic can be illogical at times, but none the worse for that. A group of Radicals, whose café was in the next street, called upon M. Lambert, to ask him if he would write them a leaflet. He received them coldly, as befitted a Royalist.

"I am, Messieurs, a philosopher, not a hurler of bombs."

"Exactly," said the spokesman. "We should like some philosophical leaflets. No crude phrasing, you understand. We want some fine literature for a change."

"Like the Encyclopedia?"

"Precisely that!"

Lambert sat down and wrote one off, stiffly, in the manner of a fashionable doctor writing a prescription for a mule's hoof. They were grateful. They paid him two hundred francs. It was a learned bit of writing, and nobody could make head or tail of it. That night Lambert polished up his best stick, went out and dined well.

Through an oversight in the matter of a license, the distributors got pinched, the leaflets were confiscated and hauled to the warehouse.

Months later, the Arrondissement decided to send out notices. Improvements were to be voted on—new pavements and a storm drain. A clerk, one of those pin-saving bureaucrats, was reminded of a lot of paper on hand, and thrift would counsel its use. So the leaflets—with M. Lambert's detached and logical exposition that concealed dynamite—were hauled out and imprinted on the reverse. Postmen delivered ten thousand to homes of every shade of political thought. There was a great rumpus over this afterwards, when it was too late. The upshot of it was that ten Syndicalists were voted into office. M. Lambert got all the praise, to his horror. He was supposed to have engineered the coup. A Machiavelli.

The Royalists called upon him, with a delegation from the Friends of the King. Would he contrive that again for the opposition?

"Impossible! We'd all go to jail."

"Well, then, would Monsieur write a monthly pamphlet for us?"

"That remains to be seen."

"Would eight thousand francs a year be a visible sum?"

It was. And between articles on zoology, plants, and Augustan ruins, M. Lambert beat the drum in his lucid and scholarly style for the cause of the Bourbons. It made no difference at the forum, where anything at the Elysée or even across the street (another Quarter) might as well be happening in China. Thereafter our Mayor lived in ease.

It was not until winter that our paths crossed, and then in a way he never suspected. For weeks I had misjudged him; thought him a sprite or an erratic, up to secret mischief. I was convinced that somebody on this floor had somehow found egress to my room when I was away at the Faisan d'Or. Half a dozen times, when opening the lower drawer of my dressing table to take out my linen, I found a handful of cheese rinds and lettuce leaves inside a ring of collars. Cantal cheese rinds.

It was either a jest, I thought, or the caprice of a senile yet diabolical mind. I put a new lock on the door. But the *apports,* as table rappers call them, still appeared. Though disturbed, not for anything would I have charged the philosopher, immersed to his neck in speculations on zoology and ruins, a mild, shy Silenus, too deeply absorbed even to scrape up a greeting as we passed on the stairs, with playing so weird a caprice upon me. No, I had not the courage.

One night, being unable to sleep, I lay reading a book, and I became aware of a movement in the room. An invisible hand might have been shaking the canvas. It was a white shape, gliding up. It slid into a hole in the ceiling. I flung myself at the bureau, looked into the drawer, and there again was a piece of rind. Not the philosopher, but a snow-white rat was the miscreant. The next day I poked into the ceiling a crust dipped in arsenic and glued a paper over the hole.

I had acted on impulse, and in a very little while I was sorry. It seemed a shabby way to treat a small creature that had done me no harm with its pranks, that had only wanted to make a nest somewhere, and that had gone to endless trouble to drag rinds and leaves through that wilderness of rafters overhead, gone down the canvas and up along the leg of the bureau into the drawer. It may, besides, have been someone's pet. I had killed it.

Somewhere, either along the Quay or at the Bird Market, I bought a white rat, a tamed one, with a black face, and after taking out the crust I turned her loose among the rafters, and thus made my *amende honorable*. For many nights I heard it scutter overhead, exploring its new world, making itself at home; then all was quiet, and I supposed it had tired and strayed elsewhere.

Before long I was introduced by the pork butcher to "our Mayor," and it became my habit to drop in one or two evenings a week. The Mayor knew more about food than I did. He had written a book on spices, and he dug it out from a pile of volumes so tumbled over and chaotic that he had to crawl through a tunnel of them to drag it out. He was very proud of the section on cloves, drawn from his wanderings in Zanzibar, whence comes most of that spice. Almost half the yield goes to the Dutch East Indies, where it goes into Kreteke cigarettes.

"From Zanzibar we went on to Madagascar," he said, sprawling in his chair with feet on a stool. "Myself and a lad of my age. We shipped on as cabin boys. Only one passenger aboard, and that was enough. The Tartar! He was the new military Governor. Nothing we did pleased him. He had the English vice of eating boiled eggs for breakfast, but they had to be fresh. We had only ten hens aboard, all too miserable to lay when we got into rough sea.

"So one morning we chipped a tiny hole at the end of an egg, dropped into it one of his shirt studs, then, after boiling, smoothed it over with wax. His stupor when he beheld his shirt stud in a spoonful of white was ample reward for our trouble. He bolted to the Captain with the egg—the Captain, mind you—and the two of them marched to the afterdeck to stare at that bewitched crate of poultry, trying to figure out which hen it was that had violated the established order regarding eggs."

The Mayor had an uncommon mind. He was a humanist with a boundless curiosity. Nothing human, nor extra-human, was alien to him. He had dug for Priam's treasure with Schliemann in Greece, and journeyed through Egypt, looking for some rare kind of mummy, with Virchow. One long shelf in his room just about sagged with pots and dog-headed jars of such age and rarity that the Louvre would have envied him.

We were sipping wine one night, when my eye espied in the corner a brass cage with a little Eiffel Tower in it, and a treadmill. Two white rats were looking at me, one perfectly white, the other with a black mask. I started.

"Ah, you have not yet seen my pets?" beamed Monsieur Lambert. He took up a cheese rind, and with it playfully scratched their backs. "This is Scaramouche, and that is Fadette.

"They are the closest friends I have in the world. I adore them. But Fadette—there is the fickle one! Once she vanished for two weeks, leaving her mate home to keep the family virtues bright while she cut up somewhere—the trull! She came back timorously. He repulsed her, even bit her on the ear.

"She has forgiven him, I think. The strange thing is that she returned a shade lighter—the ghost of herself with a black face. Change in hair coloring is not infrequent in the species, but in only two weeks' time—interesting, is it not?"

I could only nod, and feel criminal.

X

François le Grand

In the old priory days the vaulted niche in the kitchen of the Faisan d'Or had sheltered an altar. Two granite steps led one up to it from the kitchen. Inside were a long table with a carafe of wine and a few chairs, and here the chefs rested when they could leave their stoves. I recall it now with nostalgia, this club—the vista from it into the smoke-filled aisle, as from a box at an opera. The white-capped artists; the shuttling *camionettes* piled high with dishes; Sidi, the giant Senegalese dishwasher, eternally spitting cardamom seeds through teeth like flagstones; Pless, the *sommelier*, like a scarab in his coat of gold-and-emerald; and the waiters, who had the faces of croupiers, most of them, or of men grown hard in finance or politics. Often they paused to buzz-buzz into each other's ears—eyebrows uplifted as if pinned, foreheads in wrinkles, like lines ploughed in ivory.

Pless was a good friend of ours, his temperament inclining him to the cooks. He was a ponderous, mild Alsatian who kept usually to his wine cave, smoking a pipe and carving bushels of peach stones into intaglios of adorable little nudities. Sidi wore a double necklace of them underneath his shirt, and a pair on his watch fob.

The *sommelier* kept our carafe filled, and not always with *vin ordi-*

naire. The wines that François, the roast chef, and I sipped in this niche! Hessians; some gracious Moselles; once a Johannisberger from a world of pomp and ceremonial, with the dark blue seal, the highest in the Archangelic hierarchy of Cabinet wines; and again a Hermitage, perfumed amber and liqueurish, far older than the oldest chef in the Faisan d'Or. Pless salvaged these for us from the diplomatic feasts waited upon by Pierre.

François, a dwarf-like Attila, and fully as strong—he could balance a whole beef on his head and walk off with it—drank these wines in sips, squatted deep in his chair, with tongue rolling and resounding "Ah's!" He was a Breton who had passed his youth in Louisiana, and gained for himself the sobriquet of "the Creole."

The wine finished, he rolled cigarettes of fine Smyrna tobacco, like pine needles, and smoked with one eye upon the joints turning at his fire bank opposite, the flames licking and sputtering in a sullen conflagration. To François a roast was a joint roasted against an open fire, not devitalized in an iron box of an oven, and called, properly, funeral baked meats.

"Charcoal fumes shorten our lives," once declaimed a kitchen immortal, "but what matters that if we but add luster to our name and glory?" François breathed no fumes (he usually looked on from the niche), and glory he valued less than a fig. Perhaps it was because he already had it; he basked in the admiration of the kitchen, since those in the craft knew that he was one of the great inventive chefs of the world. Who else knew it? Perhaps nobody. The widest renowns being seldom the reward of superior merit, the virtuosi pass through life undiscerned save by the elect.

François' taste was impeccable. His verdict in wine, for he had a divination into the nature of that mysterious living entity, even Urbain regarded as final. He was perhaps unduly severe toward the cooks who failed to create miracles with their materials. This was understandable, for he thought them blackguards or assassins.

François, the broad-shouldered gnome, with his vast white bonnet, his hauteur, his imperial beard, who strutted with a fork as big as a Neptune's trident, was my favorite after Guido left.

"Jean-Marie," he would say, "come with me to the morgue."

So down he would go to the meat vaults. François had a sort of tunnel at the end of the icebox, coal-black and moist, where game hung, and long cuts of fillet wrapped in cheesecloth. He would pull open the door, mumble into the darkness, and smack his lips. You could see nothing there but glows of phosphorescence.

"See! Fireworks! A little more blue over the fillets, and they're ready to scream, 'Eat me'!"

Even lower in the scale than unskillful cooks he ranked persons who were ignorant of what they ate.

One autumn the spokesmen of three Powers, upon whose decision hung the destiny of the world—so precariously is our planet balanced—met at a town on the Riviera, and there they were to drink Madeira, dine, and talk for a whole week. Their names I have forgotten. From Paris were dispatched, by gracious assent of the Faisan d'Or, Messrs. Pless and François to look after all but the Treaty itself.

All went smoothly until the close of the second day. François roasted for the dinner half a young antelope. Had it been fed on fern shoots, grass, and reeds, it would have been perfect; but that dry summer in the Tyrol it had fed overlong on apple twigs and herbage that was papery rather than lush. François was distressed.

The solution was to serve it not with salt alone but with an Espagnol sauce. In a great saucepan he fried meat and bones of beef, veal and ham, with onions, celery, carrots, turnips, *fines herbes,* cloves, allspice, cannel, and pepper. Then he put in the thick *roux,* then poultry carcasses and tomatoes. It is a tedious sauce to make— a long task and involved. After two hours he put in sherry.

François tasted it. What did it lack? He had a palate for flavors as some have an ear for music. Aha, coriander!

Since all was prepared except the dessert—a soufflé of pineapple to be ovened at the last minute—he went out, mounted upon a Foreign Minister's bicycle, and pedalled into the cool air in quest of the herb which wearied the Israelites so extremely in their manna that they sighed for the fleshpots and fish of Egypt. The shops had none of it. He rode on, sniffing past many little gardens and calling out to all the old ladies sitting on their doorsteps. He bought some at last, a handful, and stuck it in his hat and pedalled home.

He went straight to that saucepan in the kitchen, and found it empty! His senses almost left him. He braced himself and walked into the dining hall.

"François," a minister plenipotentiary called out, "this is a soup finer, much finer, than any we ever tasted before."

François drew himself up with such dignity that he seemed two feet higher than his four feet nine. His voice shook with emotion.

"That, Messieurs, was an Espagnol sauce—still incomplete."

He bowed himself out, pedalled to the station, and caught the train for Paris.

"Long before anyone else," said Pless, "François knew that conference was doomed to failure."

———

François' tastes were aristocratic. He lived in a stuffy flat near the Luxembourg Gardens, clogged with books on history and gastronomics, paintings of generals and court ladies, music boxes, embroideries, and birds in cages. We used to sit in the Gardens and talk, or listen to the band brassily attacking operatic airs. He was fond of music, still unsated after a long but congenial exile in the Louisiana bayous, where his father had a tavern.

There were still celebrities in the Luxembourg. He pointed out Charles Maurras for me, and a journalist or two of the staff of *L'Action Française.* This corner was a haunt of the Royalists: the old ladies in shabby black, knitting under the foliage of the plane trees, and the elderly mustachios reading politics, or engaged in grave discussion as they walked up and down the paths. François himself, in his broad velour hat and frock coat, was both Royalist and celebrity.

He went little to the theater now; nothing he could see was as fine as what he had seen, except the Molière plays at the Odéon. As for the chefs—

"Gone narrow," he shrugged. "Unrivalled in their narrow field, yes, but beyond it—what? Too often they are trained as pastry cooks. They become not interpreters but scientists, chained to a rigid formula, like those unhappy Hindu bridegrooms wedded to trees.

"I have known British chefs—a few, mind you, no more than two or three—who were great eclectics. Did they not live in the hub of Empire, the hub of many spokes—Colonial, African, English folk cookery, and the Indian, which is Persian, Rajput, and ancient Greek and Palmyran—so that when a dish of it, wrought in honor and joyfulness, is placed before a man, he will be the richer for having dined on the art and history and poetry of fifty centuries.

"And those chefs also knew much of the Continental, and of the American, with its Deep South—unknown terrain to most of America—where flourish the turtle fricassee, orange-fed turkeys, gumbo *z'herbes,* crayfish bisque, marsh ducks *en estofade,* peppers à la Mme. Begué, crabs without chemise, and pompano cooked in a paper hat as large as a nun's.

"Even so, the North of America has its consolations. There and nowhere else must one turn for a lemon pie, or a chowder—Breton, though its ancestor was, the *chaudière* of the fishing boats. Only Maine and anglicized Quebec know how to bake the white bean. For a crockful of it, if famished on a cold winter night, I would barter all the flageolets in Provence.

"I, my young friend, am tolerance itself, and I exult in merit wherever found. Perfection may strike anywhere—like a bolt of lightning! And the man struck need not always be a Gaul! Whoever he is, he must also pay the price of perfection, which is narrowness. Balzac wrote good novels, but was an indifferent cook, for all his infatuation with the kitchen.

"As cooks, we French may have less scope, but what we are brought up to know, that we know supremely well. I often wish I could adventure a trifle at the Faisan d'Or, at least to the extent of preparing an Oyster Florentine—but what fulminations should I try! I would be run out of the premises as a traitor! Out with the *coquin* who says an oyster can be eaten cooked as well as raw. He shows a lack of confidence in our national ideals! He thumbs his nose at the sacred Tricolor!

"Of foreigners we are wary, and distrustful; though, in the kitchen, not of Italians. Italy, as the world knows, is the one country with the inward conviction that art is really supreme."

In such vein talked François, my mentor, who had traversed oceans, and in the voyaging lost not a grain of his native virtue. He talked with hands flying, stick hooked on a thumb—the kobold eloquent, his voice a massive basso. He paused, and sniffed.

"Aha, we are coming to the Rue Mouffetard! Somewhere about here is a bottle!"

The nose that had inhaled the scent of magnolias and the tepid, odorous breath of the Louisiana bayous never led him wrongly in the alleys of Paris. Into the Rue Mouffetard we entered. Its air sparkled with frost under a chill and blue December sky. A week of mild heat and nights of plumping rain in Brittany had garnished the stalls with the splendor of early vegetables: hampers of endives, truffles, mushrooms, and cress; a plenitude of herbs; and crates of geese so fat that ancient kitcheners, leaning on sticks, dewdrop on nose and coat collars turned up, gazed at them lost in dreams. They might have strayed into the Land of Cockaigne.

"Ha!" breathed François, in a reverential sigh.

The earth spirit, in accord with the gods of the hearth and spit, had been bounteous. There were beeves, this side of deification, crowned and hung with ribbands. Sole and whiting, and Devon lobsters with forearms like Vulcan's, were heaped up in a salt-encrusted baskets, on frozen seaweed. It was a month notable in cheeses: in Camembert, Pont l'Évêque, Excelsior, and in Brie now as plump as cream tarts. Plover, woodcock, and partridge were strung in festoons, their neck feathers a-glitter in the winter sunlight. The vision and splendor of feasts-to-be stirred the heart already moved by the pounding of the bells in the steeple of St.-Médard.

We turned into the Rue Tournefort, and in the bleak edifice where Balzac's Père Goriot lived, we entered a small café. I was half frozen, and a little sad. It was an empty December for me. A letter had apprized me of a loss: Rémy, still in Switzerland, but on a higher Alp and in a bigger Ghismont hotel, was to marry Freda before the year's end.

"The wine," said François.

A bottle stopped with sealing wax was brought him, and he poured it out. It was a red wine of Noirmoutier, the island off the coast of Vendée—a crusted, vinous, and dark wine, redolent of the seaweed ash flung upon it to foster the bloom on its grape; a sea melodrama of a wine, the Atlantic tang of it a sword slash through velvet.

"A home wine," said François. "I lived there a long time. I close my eyes and again behold the white surf and the black monastery, and the road across from the mainland; the road dripping and moss-green, visible only on low tide. That was where Briand, dozing in his chair, his vest white with cigar ash, hid away from the world, dreaming and sipping the red wine of Noirmoutier.

"Madame, another bottle, and some figs!"

She brought us a string of them, the Bourjasotte Grise, hanging a score to the string from a nail on the wall—hard outside, but with jelly-like pulp, aromatic and winy. They were from Provence, my home.

As I bit into them, I dined with phantoms. The filaments of one's taste buds stretch into the past. Their ends are shaken by memories. And if there is fragrance, the past—even the forgotten parts of it—enfolds one instantly. A whiff of saffron, the smell of pastry in the oven, and one is a child again. The true pleasure in eating comes not from the gratification of the senses as in the awakening of a subliminal faculty. Saint Francis, who knew the delicious honey of the slope where he played when small, knew whereof he spoke when he gave sustenance of truth in a sermon to the Poor Clares, and called it "spiritual bee-bread."

"In the Bastille," said François, peeling another fig and talking as if to himself, "is a small cook shop, not clean, but very good. I sometimes go there with a friend, a botanist who is half English. He eats there, on summer days when it is raining, a rhubarb tart. A sort of compulsion.

"He eats it slowly, then puts down his fork, and is bowed over the plate in a kind of trance. He described it as a feeling of bliss, of warm sheltering, as if he were very young and protected.

"It was, he told me, only lately that he understood. The root of it was exposed to him suddenly when he was eating the tart very hot. Back in his early years, when he was an orphan living with an aunt in Vendée, and asleep one afternoon, she woke him and told him to go to the rhubarb patch to see a nest of singing birds she had just found. He dashed out, looked at the birds, and was shaken with excitement and a glad rapture. He had an umbrella, for there was both rain and a burst of hot sunshine. The rain drummed on large rhubarb leaves, and they steamed. There was also the roar of surf on the beach. He was very young, you understand—five or six— new in a world that was magical. Children are not the young of the human race. They are of a race apart, and have different and very intense feelings. The mother bird was singing on a twig. The smell of the leaves—"

François refilled his glass. "In itself, rhubarb can be, in some circumstances, good. What is it, a fruit or a vegetable?"

"A weed, I think, but not necessarily a damned weed. You had better ask your botanical friend."

XI

Musk Ox and Sherbet

The Faisan d'Or was deep in her seasonal lull, four of her banquet halls shrouded; Urbain and Monsieur Paul, in an Anglophile mood, were poking about inns along the Thames, and for a month were to be lost in the Hebrides, looking for a certain wild Highlander whose pot still had never known the locks of the exciseman. I had been left with some vaguely denoted powers, and the occupancy of Monsieur Paul's sanctum. The staff was impressed, I think. The laundress brought in my linen so heavily starched that it was painful to wear; my bonnet was whiter, stiffer than before, a foot higher—a cloud atop a funnel.

I was having my breakfast of coffee and a brioche, with a copy of *Candide* propped against the cruet. Seeing an article closing with the signature "Lambert," I read it, as I did everything by that exquisite author of grocery catalogues, who nourished his spirit on the richness of the antique past. Some Russians, his story said, exploring a terminal moraine above the Arctic Circle, had dug deeper than usual in their hunt for rocks; they chipped out some bones, then a brace of musk oxen, perfectly preserved. More oxen were below, in that eternal icebox.

This was the peg on which our Academician had hung an essay

remarkable for its learning and charm of expression. Pleistocene man had a thin time of it, by all accounts. The climate was not at its best, and when the earth shook under the mammoths that trotted past, he hid in his cave. There were also sabertooth tigers, and lions twice the size of the breed at the zoo. As often as not, he was the hunted and not the hunter; he dined on roots, for he had no other weapon than a chunk of flint. If luck favored him, he could knock over a leathery bird, or some kind of hare.

I was pondering over this when François lounged in.

"Old fellow," he shouted, "that's fatal—wearing a hat that high. You know what happens to a chef whose hat is too—too altitudinous! He gets flung out!"

"You ought to be wearing it, François. The second in command, you know."

He grinned. We both knew I had been put in as a stopgap in this dull season, and that Monsieur Paul, though secure in his tenure of office, and the *doyen* of his profession, regarded him as the only possible rival in the esteem of the patrons.

"It's quiet, Jean-Marie. Only half the staff here, and unless we get some excitement we'll have to go into the streets and whip up a riot." He poured himself a glass of brandy and sank heavily into a chair. "It's even stupider than it was last year. I should have gone fishing."

"Read this," I said. "It's Mayor Lambert in his best vein."

He read it, gulped his brandy down, then paced the room, agitatedly polishing his pince-nez. He tried to speak, but his will could bring forth only a deep breath and gesticulations. Another glass, and he stared, blinking, at the article; then he tore feebly at his neckcloth.

"Jean-Marie—think of it! A million years! That musk-ox beef has been pretty well hung! If we could only get a joint of it!"

"Melun-Perret ought to hear of this," I laughed.

"I have an idea!" the Creole broke in. "A Pleistocene banquet! That would be something. Think of what it would mean to the Faisan d'Or. Astounding *réclame*, for one thing, with the moral of a vast increase in business. How that would please Urbain!"

"It would be a novelty." I wrote on a pad. "Pleistocene banquet. Soup, a *potage* of musk-ox tail. Then a prime roast of musk ox, a double-rack, with King Edward the Seventh trimmings—garnish, sauce, and so forth. Vegetable, purée of fossil moss."

My Creole rubbed his hands. "And some fossils from the Sorbonne, tottering professors, very learned, with beards parted in the middle! A banquet for archaeologists. The very notion of it, my young friend, is staggering!"

"We must first catch our musk ox, of course," I said. "A mere detail. I shall discuss it with Melun-Perret. He will regard it as a most prodigious idea, such a dinner. Also," I warmed up, "it seems to me that our Mayor is deserving of the Legion of Honor ribbon, and this would bring his name into cosmic renown. Alas, that so great a scholar should have been doomed to obscurity through his brains!

"And by the way, François, it is his birthday on Thursday next. We shall have a little dinner at his place, and you will cook it."

And so we were agreed. I dispatched a telegram to Georges at his house in the Champs Élysées. He was so pleased at the notion that he postponed for a week the installation of a new and beautiful Grecian in an apartment that he maintained discreetly elsewhere.

We were eight in all. Mayor Lambert had brightened his flat, dusted his books, arranged flowers on the trestle-board table in an alcove, and brought in three Academicians. The kitchen was a dark cupboard with two gas burners under a grid, three or four saucepans, and a spoon or two.

"We shall have," said François, "one of those small dinners, appropriate to the *décor*. And not so much phenomenal as not easy to forget. Something Creole, let us say. A Jambalaya."

He boiled up some rice, sluiced it with cold water, and let it dry. In butter he fried a few cloves of garlic, two onions, and a green pepper, chopped into bits, then four peeled tomatoes. These and the rice he combined in a saucepan with a pint of cooked shrimps, pepper, salt, and cayenne. He covered it to simmer for half an hour, with an occasional moistening of stock and, at the end, a tablespoonful of sassafras powder.

It was dark, hot, and aromatic, and after the bland consommé struck a harmonic chord with the cooled Chablis. We sat framed against books of red and black leather and oiled vellum, the beards of the Academicians and our host gleaming in the luster of the shaded lamp hanging above the table. The Mayor sat at the end, formal in an embroidered green waistcoat, a row of clay jars on the shelf above his head.

The food was pungent; it was novel; the eaters were silent, as if they experienced through it the sense of a withdrawal from the common life. A small Academician who was eighty, and as remote from the world as if he were in old Assyria, smiled like an infant.

"It is like a *paella* I had once in Seville. But this has a strangeness, with green shadows, a breath like an emanation of the jungles, perhaps African. The hypnosis of a flavor, gentlemen, partakes of a spiritual revelation. For the moment we are in a Louisiana bayou."

He rested his head against two high volumes of Pliny, his bearded face, in the shadow, as white as a cloud and beautiful.

We had plenty of Chablis, then a sharp-tasting salad of greens. François, very gently so as not to disturb the serene talk, slipped to the corner where the kitchen was, and I after him. He had come early to prepare the brandy pudding, and it was cooled now in the box of cracked ice.

He had, I recall, creamed the yolks of eight eggs with two cupfuls of sugar and two cupfuls of brandy, thickened it in a double boiler. He removed it from the fire and cut in the stiffened egg whites. When this was cool, he worked in a tablespoonful of old marmalade and a quart of whipped cream, and many dashes of the orange bitters they know in New Orleans bar rooms. He allowed it to set in a compote dish paved and walled with macaroon cakes.

François flicked in a thumb and licked it. *"Dites moi, ma mère,"* he hummed as he carried the dessert to the table.

It was a rich and gracious finish, yet subdued enough to keep vivid the excellence of all that had gone before. We lingered over it so that the coffee was embraced in its sunset.

Georges opened a bottle of pale *eau de vie* so ethereal that we breathed its aroma at the plop of the cork. Lambert took down eight of the clay jars, and after they were rinsed—since we had no more glasses—Georges filled them with the cognac.

We smoked Larranagas; we inhaled and sipped *eau de vie* from the small earthenware jars. Georges, his bland and candid eye rolling benevolently at us through the smoke, got out pencil and envelope, and planned the banquet for us.

"A month from tonight. Item: full haunch of musk ox. Item: fossil moss, if edible." He rolled his perfecto and scribbled. "Item: some Pleistocene sweetbreads for a *vol-au-vent*. How's that for a start?"

"But that will take months," said Lambert.

"Four days at the outside, I assure you. I'll send my plane and sky chauffeur up there. He'll take along some vodka and a case of Port, for our Russian friends will need some cheering in that gloom. Anything else we can get out of the Pleistocene?"

"Nothing," said the Mayor. "But I know where we can get some old rice. Four measures, at least. In sealed urns, dug up in the ruins of Palmyra. That's a quantity, you see. More than you'd get from a hundred mummies with rice in their clutch."

Georges murmured with approbation.

"We're getting somewhere. Now, the wine."

"We'll find none so old," said the Academician. "Lucky for us. My Bulgar colleague, Professor Vuletich, gave me a taste of that Opimian, bottled in the year Caius Gracchus was slain in the revolt of the plebs. It has a lump of purple enamel. We made a tincture in alcohol, and had a teaspoonful apiece. It tasted like ink. *Vinum insaluberrimum.* But there it was, wine already old before Rome was an empire."

"Vuletich, where is he?"

"In Sofia."

"I'll go there in a plane myself and bring him and the Opimian."

"If that precious, that unique, relic should fall—"

"Then we shall both perish with it!"

"What I want to know," said François patiently, "is, how many will be there?"

It took longer to draw up the list than to invent the Pleistocene menu. Not all scientists approve of every other scientist in the world. Mayor Lambert suggested twenty names. The old Academician winced at all of them, as if he had bitten into a persimmon. So with twenty other names.

"Well, then," said Georges, "let us have other than malefactors."

He sipped delicately from his little jar. It was of a pagan loveliness, with lip flared as in a Grecian lamp, and a design in faded red on its black, glazed body, so thin and time-hardened that the liqueur swirling in it gave forth an elfin ring.

"A fitting ceramique for the brandy," he murmured. "Let me congratulate you on your pots."

"You have discernment, M'sieu." Mayor Lambert held a light to a fresh cigar. "Spiteri, the Maltese archaeologist, found these in a tomb. They are Pompeiian tear jars."

By midnight we were agreed on the choice of guests. Twelve in all, taken from the first list. The brandy gone, we left and I said good night to the diners before their taxicabs at the curb. François was the last to go. He smote his chest, then stared at me.

"The dessert!" he shouted. "The Pleistocene dessert! What shall we have for that?"

He leaped in, the door slammed like a pistol shot, and the taxicab sped in pursuit of Georges and the Academicians.

———

This banquet, where should it be held? The major-domo was for the Talleyrand salon; Pierre for the Blue Room, with its Gobelins and plush chairs, its Fragonards and ormolu. Urbain's assistant was for screening off a corner of the great dining room, where a door led directly into the kitchen. I was talking with him and François in the crypt, when light came upon me.

"I have it! The cellar!"

We clattered down the stairs. Across from the wine cave was an unused chamber as dark as an oubliette, empty except for a half dozen broken hogsheads. I caught up a lantern and fetched it in. Cobbles bulged from the walls of crude and solid masonry; the paving was of large flagstones; the rafters had been hacked into shape with an adze.

"Is this Pleistocene enough?"

The chamber was thirty yards square, and its fireplace could have housed a coach. François struck a match and peered up the chimney. The draft was perfect. He vowed he could hear owls up above, in the trees. The place might have been built to purpose for the tryst with the musk ox.

"To think I've been in the Faisan d'Or since I was a *piccolo,* and never once heard of it," said Urbain's assistant.

His energy was prodigious. He had the cellar washed out; hung candelabra in the shape of cartwheels from the rafters; put a grid and turnspit in the fireplace; set up rough pine tables and chairs. Thirty chairs, not twelve: the Minister of Instruction was coming as a guest of Georges, and since that made it a diplomatic affair five Senators had had to be invited. The *chefs de cuisine* of the Roi Nantois, the Dauphin-Splendide, and the Noel Peters—these I invited on behalf of the Faisan d'Or.

The dungeon was thrown open. The light came from flames in braziers; the floor was carpeted with yew twigs. Heading the guests who filed in between rocks, as into a cave, were the Minister of Instruction and the Rector of the Sorbonne.

François entered, with him an upright, small man in white mustachios, with puckered, wise face, a frock coat and a rosette in his lapel. A supreme moment! Ah, Monsieur Paul, you should have been there! The guests rose in homage. Flashlights blazed. It was the great Maître Escoffier himself, writer of *La Guide Culinaire Moderne,* who bowed to the assemblage, and with grace seated himself between Melun-Perret and the ducal Doctor di Valmonte.

The flower of Gaul's culinary genius sat in that chair, smiling, chatting urbanely, in the person of this immortal, over whom hung an aura of unreality proper to legendary beings. Had he not, this inventor of Peach Melba and an octave of new sauces, been chef to Napoleon Third? Had he not been Bismarck's first prize of war at the Fall of Sedan? Had not the post of *chef des cuisines* of the Hotel Cecil been accorded him at the express wish of King Edward the Seventh?

History, perhaps, does not record another such instance of persons so illustrious in the fields of diplomacy, the arts, and pure learning gathering underground to dine on primordial viands, nor to dine anywhere with such anticipation, zest, and urbane hilarity. The musk ox yielded to the tooth, and the soufflé of cormorant eggs—cormorants are still extant, but look as if they ought to be extinct, and the zoo had been kind enough to supply us with some eggs of this fowl—went down gullets as smoothly as the oil flowed down Aaron's beard. No diner writhed on the floor in attitudes worthy of Dante. And there was cognac—a great plenty of cognac.

The dinner was high in merit, considering the obstacles, but far higher in singularity. Fire thrummed on the hearth, and on the spit a haunch of musk ox revolved slowly, François basting it with ladles of sour cream. He had marinated it two days and nights. The immensity of that haunch which had propelled the beast over pastures when Europe was a tundra fresh from the receding ice cap was enough to inspire the diners with awe, with the most oppressive feelings of antiquity. It did, until the post-prandial champagne was poured out, to go along with the wafers of smoked Arctic dolphin on thin rice cakes.

The Palmyran rice, brought in by the old Academician, had resembled nothing so much as buckshot. We had ground it up with the fossil moss, a vegetable like hard coral, steeped it a fortnight in hot water, and made batter cakes. We had much left for a soufflé made with the beaten whites of cormorant eggs.

François carved the haunch with a sword-shaped blade, from which the slices fell, handsome and succulent, as dark as the red Argentine beef, onto plates so hot that the plates sputtered with the juice. The Duc di Valmonte, hero of a dozen banquets almost as epochal, sat as if hypnotized.

From stone jugs the waiters poured out a wine tinctured with the enamel dissolved in spirits, brought safely in Melun-Perret's plane from Sofia. It had a taste of museums, naturally.

Then followed quenelles of musk-ox liver à la maréchale, with Finnish cucumbers, aromatic as smelts, ripened in the long midnight sun. Then a salad of sea moss, cockles, and roe—all from the Arctic. Then a dessert of sherbet, made of a large chunk of fossil ice, as old as the musk ox itself, and coal-black. I had rendered it to powder and whipped it up with lime juice and syrup. Very handsome it looked under the soft lights.

Our *sommelier* brought in jeroboams of Perrier-Jouet, that poured out flashing amber and green, like the fountains at Versailles. Musicians came in to play flutes, bassoons, and hautboys—archaic, distant music, yet fanciful and gay.

The crowds outside the Faisan d'Or were enormous, for the journals had lifted interest still higher; and there were searchlights and an ambulance, sent down by the *Excelsior* newspaper, which had first claim to reports of disaster. Behind the rope in the cellar were spectators and reporters. Flashlights blinked every second, and the place filled with smoke. The Academicians, clutching at their throats, coughed and wheezed. Pierre, to save us from asphyxiation, dashed in with electric fans. Newsreel cameras whirred. Journalists climbed over the rope to interview Georges Melun-Perret, who, instead, led them to speak with Mayor Lambert, sitting at the head of the table, though his lapel was bare of decoration. They scribbled endless notes.

After that, speeches: first Mayor Lambert, then the Minister of Instruction. Then the fragile-ivory old Academician, with fingers plunging into his snuffbox, gave a speech, and it was the oddest of all.

"Fellow citizens," he began, "the Pleistocene was an intractable age. I assume that was the era of which we have been the guests.

"Of all its fauna the musk ox was the most admirable. One can only regret that it was overwhelmed by avalanches. I hope that explorers, instead of hunting in the boreal regions for beds of coal, or future airplane fields, will discover deep strata of musk oxen, inexhaustible mines of beef, enough to keep man well fed for twenty generations!

"As an archaeologist I should like to praise tonight's particular haunch. It proves that the bovine species was even before the dawn of antiquity perfect; that it had attained perfection when mankind was indistinguishable from orangutans. Man's defects are a scandal of the globe. Theologians have little good to say of him. Perhaps, through wars, he is headed for extinction. But—but—one good thing must be said for this grotesque but often well-meaning biped: he invented wine!

"Messieurs!" He lifted his glass. "To Noah, who first planted the grape!"

And that was the toast. The Academician sat down heavily. He smiled blissfully into space. He was really very drunk.

We heard much about the Pleistocene the next day, and several days after—perhaps too much. Enough Academicians, gourmets, scientists, and deputies to consume a herd of musk oxen were irritated at having been overlooked. The papers broke out in dithyrambs on the banquet, and printed every detail and speech. The Faisan d'Or might have been the only restaurant in Paris, in the world, and François the chef of the age. You saw him in the newsreels; you heard him on the radio; he was notorious. The Club des Cent, that premier gastronomic council, gave him a luncheon in the Faubourg St. Honoré. As for Mayor Lambert, both the *Candide* and the *Nouvelles Littéraires* declared that a ribbon must be bestowed upon him at once.

Patronage at the Faisan d'Or doubled overnight. It increased as the week went on. Then Monsieur Paul came back suddenly from his English tour, stalked through the kitchen to his office, and called me in.

"I fail, Monsieur Gallois," he said coldly, dashing his hand on a pile of newspapers spread out on his desk, "I fail to understand the meaning of all this."

He turned over one cartoon after another. There was François grilling steaks for Stone Age men shivering amid icebergs. There was François shaking hands with senators—and with the immortal Escoffier himself, an honor reserved for generals, statesmen, and ruling heads.

"And this—and this!"

Monsieur Paul looked up at me with the hurt and reproachful eyes of a spaniel that had been treated harshly.

"Monsieur," I said, "I began it for the good of the Faisan d'Or. In a way, it was a jest that paid, and I am sorry if—"

"Ring the bell for François!"

I did. As François moved in, with his slow, barge-like gait, wiping his hands upon his apron, I withdrew and closed the door. His summoning was indicative of Monsieur Paul's sharp displeasure. I looked about me, but saw that no one else in the kitchen was aware trouble was afoot, for they were all intent on their tasks.

Through the garden door, which was ajar, I saw Jules kneeling amid his pots of tarragon and coriander and basil. Beyond his herbs he strayed rarely. For this close with its heap of rocks, vestiges of a Cistercian chapel, grown over with fennel and basil, and the small lodge where he had his room, he had a monkish attachment. He found in it a permanence and an enfolding, warm content that armored him against the harsh, outside world. He saw me through the herbs, and he shook his head sorrowfully.

"Ah, Jean-Marie," he might have said, "you will be going back to your nougats."

François was still in the office, and his measured rumbling went through the kitchen like thunder. He was resigning. In his demissory address, his arm going up and down, he was giving each sentence the weight, the edge of an artist as matchless in invective as in the roasting of meats. He spoke with deliberation in a French that was as bookish as a speech at the Academy. At intervals he gave his deep chest a thump like the impact of a battering ram. He had, he said, created history. And it was true. Habitués of the Faisan d'Or measured history, not by battles and reigns, but by dinners, banquets, and the triumphs of its artists in the kitchen.

"And now, Monsieur Paul, personally—"

Both François' arms went up into the air, and vibrated. He threw aside declamation, and went in for pure feeling, unpacking his heart in a bayou Creole with the miasma of Africa upon it. His language would have frozen the scalp of a drill sergeant. In the garden Jules put hands over his ears. The Singhalese leaned his broom against the wall and shook with unaffected terror. Monsieur Paul—we could see him through the glass partition—bowed over the desk, covering his face. François emerged. The door clicked behind him. He adjusted his neckcloth, gave it a light pat, and strode off.

Clear it was from his swagger and the rake of his bonnet over an eyebrow, that for this phoenix, this paragon of chefs, there was no more room at the Faisan d'Or.

His Pleistocene laurels still fresh, François betook himself to the Roi Nantois, and instantly was accorded a rank as high as Monsieur Paul's. Fortunate was the Roi Nantois, fortunate, too, its shareholders as well as its patrons, for it was soon to be emblazoned in the *Guide Michelin* with the rating of three stars. Perhaps I should add, with such tincture of modesty as might seem fit, that on the day after François' arrival I was myself installed there as master *saucier,* and supervisor of the roasts and fish.

As for Mayor Lambert, the upshot of the musk-ox feast was that he was invited to deliver five lectures on the Stone Age, and in the spring was given his decoration.

France honors those who in the fields of learning and the arts heap further luster upon her national glory. She seizes upon them with jealous possession. "France," says Balzac, "drinks the brains of men as savagely as she once chopped off their heads."

Perhaps, in the Golden Age to come, France may even honor a chef. . . .

XII

From Overseas

The fortunes of a great restaurant are no less variable than those of men, of empires, or of wine, whose glory depends on the vintage, a chance matter of bacteria and sunlight. The heyday of the Roi Nantois coincided with the regime of François. Its income rose with its prestige. In the same year the Club des Cent and the Saintsbury Club of London dined under our roof, and there were minor affairs, like banquets to kings and envoys, beyond count. Pierre joined us, bringing along our friend the *sommelier* and his cabinet of peach-stone nudities. The Faisan d'Or was undamaged by these and other forays on its personnel; for several remarkable men breathed in its kitchen still, and tradition is fruitful of talent.

None of these, perhaps, not even Jules, was greater than our swart Anteus from the bayous. His technique was masterful and original. His most intricate dishes appeared simple. In taste he was inclusive. He was like the philosopher who all his life moved zealously from one position to another in his quest for the eternal truth, and found it in tolerance. For the old schools and the masters like Francatelli, Soyer, and Escoffier, he had that extreme reverence which in the artist is so often allied with a limitless and gentle skepticism.

"Perhaps," he would say, twirling a saucepan over the flame, "the truth is elsewhere. What do I know? We shall assume that this will be damned good."

One saying of his, which I find in my notebook, should be chiselled in immemorial bronze: "Underseasoning is the subtlest emphasis. But not all dishes deserve to be subtle."

He may have had in mind his Sauce Béarnaise, nutty and buttery, with its surprising and exquisite second and third responses on the palate, like colors on tempering steel. And his sauce for barbecued mutton, with its raucous, torchlight, wild grandeur, inspired by some childhood memory of a picnic in the bayous. He ranged far. Who will forget his variant of Shrimps à la Mirabeau, a dish that secured New Orleans firmly in the affectionate regard of himself and his patrons? The Roi Nantois became, though honestly French, a clearinghouse of wonders. François held that a true racial dish should effect an instant rapport between the eater and the land of its origin. I have often wondered about this. Would a bite into an Esterhazy steak give one as vivid an insight into Hungary as two chapters of Maurus Jokai? Or a plate of haggis transpose one as instantly into the Highlands as a spring of music on bagpipes? Eaters capable of such experience with each champ of the jaws are as rare as true mystics.

He drifted into the kitchen of the Roi Nantois occasionally, this elderly, large, gruffish man in tweeds, Casson, the friend of François, with his nose like a strawberry dipping into a creamy mustache. A friend of the house, he had always dined there. He had been in Paris so long that he felt he had never lived elsewhere, and we were surprised when we learned he was an Englishman, though his mother was French.

But once he talked of his boyhood in Sussex, of a meat pudding he had in a farmhouse, spooned out to him. Sometimes the aroma and texture of it came back to him like some insistent dream. Perhaps it was a dream. But Sussex was unexcelled for its boiled puddings.

"It is, they say," François murmured. "What do I know?"

The second, or perhaps the third, year, François found himself in England. The house dispatched him there indulgently, to look at game, the Downland sheep, and other very English things, drink ale, eat tarts, and shake hands with officials in travel bureaus. Parisian chefs are as much at home in England as English acrobats are in France.

"This Sussex, is it near by?"

It was, they told him, and a pleasant county it was. And as for the puddings—well, he could eat his way through Pevensey, Bognor, and so forth, and find out for himself. So he went, and in a hamlet near Lewes, at an old coaching inn, one market day when the place was full of drovers, a pudding came before him, a *sine qua non* of puddings, steaming like Vesuvius. The exile in tweeds was right. It was more than half a dream. The inn had been making it for two hundred and seventy years.

"It's nowt a recipe," said the woman doggedly. "It's a boiling in the wash-house copper. You light the coals at six, and boil 'un until noon."

François bought tawny port for the landlord and the vicar in the parlor, double-ale for the gaffers in the taproom, and gin for the lady in the wash house. He praised everything from the steeple of the church to the interesting tavern kittens. Obduracy gave way before his charm, and erelong the recipe, older than Cromwell, almost as old as the Magna Charta, and piously withheld from the American tourists, was in his head. So were the fumes of the port. He walked down the road in the April sunshine. How enchanting was rural England, quite up to Dickens! He smiled hazily at the succulent lambs capering in the meadows, and inhaled the fresh, wild tang of mint. The larks were melodious. He toppled blissfully asleep into the ditch.

When he awoke he was in an immensely soft bed, waited upon by an apple-cheeked nurse. For two days they detained him in the hospital. Because he had stolen the recipe of the village pudding? He was wary, but he signed a harmless paper, got a three-pound check, and was solicitously set free. Some charabanc had broken a wheel on the road, upset, and spilled its passengers on top of him in the ditch, and he had been gathered up as good as dead.

It is not everybody's dish, King Hal's rump steak and kidney pudding, as François named it. It is opulent, Saxon, and baronial, and must be approached in no careless mood. François assembled it before our eyes in the kitchen, and, with the exile in tweeds and Georges, there we dined at midnight, five of us.

Sussex may frown at my disclosure, but the Roi Nantois will be indulgent. François mixed a pound of flour with half its quantity in finely ground suet, a large teaspoonful of baking powder, as much chopped parsley, and seasoning of salt and black pepper. Making a thick paste with water, he lined a bowl and kept aside enough for the lid. Within he placed two pounds of rump steak and as much of beef kidney, cut into shavings. Then a dozen oysters, a half pound of field mushrooms, five split hardboiled eggs. Then seasonings, a tablespoonful of parsley, a chopped onion, whole black peppers, half a dozen cloves, a pinch of mace. Then a cupful of claret, a dash of Worcestershire, and enough hot water to fill up to the brim. The paste lid, moistened at the edge, goes on. Then the bowl is capped with a sheet of parchment. A cloth is tied on under the rim, the corners knotted together on top, and the pudding is plunged into boiling water, to simmer without let-up for about five hours, never less than four.

The Roi Nantois improved on Sussex, as you may perceive, and to hunt for its equal in England would be useless. The kidney is more salient; the paste can induce no torpor, however genial; the inclusion of the wine and spices give it the warmth and glow of a yuletide fire.

The general run of our patrons knew it not. Nor did the British tourists who thought that, being in France, they ought to have a mousse of something. All except a group of six or seven: a bishop, a retired admiral, and their quiet friends, bull-doggy, gray men, who dined on it twice a year, making a night of it. They brought nobody else. They smoked briars and sipped hot gin and water, and talked with a faraway look in their eyes, as of men who guard a secret. They lived on the Riviera, I think, but the Roi Nantois was for them forever a part of England.

—

Casson, my friend in tweeds, leaned back and lighted his charred briar. His gruffness had vanished with the soup; and we had dined well, as we always did at Chez Raban, on trout, a ragout of hare, and a salad. He glanced through the shadows, and as he puffed he gave a nod here and there, benignly. A huge drayman, his red moon of a face divided by a black mustache bent over his plate, his temples veined in strong-jawed athleticism, his cheeks and eyes bulging, responded with a wave of his knife. He was eating with a slow, gloating, and healthy voracity. It was a wonder he saw Casson or anything else save the viands before him.

Chez Raban was a hangout of draymen, of vegetable buyers, and of wine coopers, stained and perfumed like their own casks. It was the least cleanly restaurant near the Botanical Gardens; its clientele was male, and dined in shirt sleeves; its cookery, for the charge, highly commendable. Two girls waited on the tables. Raban, a little mummy of a fellow, toiled at a stove against the wall, his fingers darting with airy swiftness. They moved over saucepans, they hovered over the steams and heats, and, truth ascertained, they withdrew, delicately, like butterflies recoiling as from the tangibility of brick, or an iron wall. Those fingers were Raban's antennae.

"Damn!" snorted Casson. "I can't see a thing from here—not a bloody thing!" He peered across the room over his glasses. "Merciful heavens!" Then, "Raban!" he called out, irritably.

Raban sped to him. "What," asked Casson in a whisper, "what did you give that ruffian tonight. What has he got there on his plate—that unworthy boor?"

"Ah, it is a *navarin* of mutton, M'sieu. A *printanier*!" Raban grinned toothlessly at us, rubbing his hands.

Casson gave a snort that would have done credit to an enraged boar at the zoo. "But the turnips, man! Where did you get them? Aren't they the little Teltower turnips?"

"Precisely, M'sieu. It is quite evident that M'sieu is a connoisseur in turnips. Perhaps even a botanist!"

"Raban, you are fittingly named!" said Casson. (And I should explain it was not a very good pun, though "Raban" is underworld or

Apache jargon for a rope halter, or noose.) "Now why is it he gets a *printanier,* and I didn't?"

"Ah, but you see, M'sieu, Grasset brought them in himself tonight. Only a hatful. They've just come into Les Halles, where he works."

"Pardon," said my friend. "And if there's any left, I wish you'd keep them for my luncheon tomorrow. And please give my compliments to M'sieu Grasset."

As the owner went over to deliver the message, Casson murmured with interest. He knew the tastes of everyone Chez Raban. He often dined here even when flush after receiving his monthly check. Had it not been for those checks from England—his intellect alone, fine botanist though he was, would have brought him to poverty—he could not have been a patron of the Roi Nantois.

"A surprising fellow, Grasset," he remarked, "though a rough Apache to the eye. He is passing rich, also; owns the dray and horses with which he trucks beef and cabbages for Les Halles. He has not lost grip with the soil. Out at Grisy-Suisnes he has a little hidden farm that earns him not a sou, but gives his soul all it craves. He is rose-mad. He dreams of roses while his truck rattles over the cobbles in the slums at night.

"Do you know how beautiful a Damask rose can be? I never did until I saw that drayman's garden walled by yews—a place of visions, full of the rustling of dryads."

Casson took a long sip of *marc,* and shrugged. "Nostalgia for the earth," he said. "In my calling, one finds many in thrall to it, and they are to be envied.

"Once I was in Philadelphia—my first visit—and I gave a talk at a college on what we are doing here in the Jardin des Plantes, and the work of some of its old professors, like Buffon and Lamarck. The people of that city were most hospitable. For a month or longer I was quite in the hands of garden lovers and students of esoteric horticulture, herbs and simples and their legends. So many of them were Quakers, all most kind and helpful, and I kept busy lecturing before one little herbal society after another.

"One afternoon I spoke at Chester, and when I got back to my hotel a letter was awaiting me. An invitation. From a Mr. Vignal, and delivered by hand. A very nice letter, saying how deeply interested he had been in my talks, and asking if I would dine with him that night. He seemed assured I would come. It happened that I had two or three other invitations for the night, and one I had halfway accepted. But something about this letter held me. He spoke about herbs and plants in a strain of exaltation, of fanaticism, almost. And that decided me. I have a curious liking for fanatics if their devotion—whether to artifacts, flints, Siamese cats, spinet music, the ancient trade routes of Africa, ghosts—is of the harmless and intense sort. Their passionately extreme interest is often the outcome of a revelation, or an experience that is valid to themselves. It may even be communicable. I could do with a spark of it.

"I changed my clothes and waited. Mr. Vignal came—a vigorous, large man, weatherbeaten, with crinkly eyes and a Swedish accent. We drove out in threatening weather, drove for twenty miles, the end of the journey in rain and black fog. A very quiet man, hardly anything to say, but I felt that he was an amateur gardener who had not been very long in this region, hardly more than a year. We turned off a road, and he opened a large iron portal that clanged behind us like the gate of a prison. The driveway was steep; it wound through grounds that must have been landscaped in the extreme. I couldn't see a damn thing except clumps of trees and bushes. Lilacs, mostly, and now and then I got the scent of a fir. The trees were innumerable.

"What an estate! At the end of a colonnade of firs the car stopped. Here was a house that I could barely see in the glim of a lantern in the portico. We hurried in through the rain.

"Behind the marble-trimmed hall, like an office, was the living room. It was small, simply furnished, with books on the walls, hundreds of books, and a cheerful fire in the grate. We sat before it, our fists around a hot drink, while brisk Mrs. Vignal chatted and spread the dinner table.

"It was not unlike a modest farmhouse, this place. Bits of fir, larch cuttings, vine, and flowers on the shelves; pine cones, lumps of bark, and specimens of wood on the side table, which had an array of specimen jars and a microscope.

"The dinner came on. Very sensible, very French; a gigot of mutton in a casserole, with buttered haricots, a salad of lettuce and chives. The Vignals' daughter joined us: a brown-haired girl of about fifteen, as quiet as her father, but with preternatural, almost sullen, gravity. How well they were bringing her up! She brought hot bread from the oven. And from a cupboard among the books she fetched a dark bottle of wine. How did that bit of flotsam, that Domaine de Chevalier, tinged with antiquity, drift to him, do you suppose? Vignal knew, and the ghost of a smile hovered about his thin lips as he poured it out, with precision, but generously, into our thick tumblers. Then we had a crag of herb cheese, aged in some dry cellar, water biscuits, and a musky pear. It was a far better dinner than I deserved.

"The table cleared, we sat about the fire of oak logs. It was late summer, but the fogs from the Susquehanna can often be cool at this altitude. The girl brought us coffee, bubbling hot, with the tang of chicory. Will the French ever cease to be grateful for this one result of the English blockade in Napoleonic times, when coffee was scarce and chicory cheap? We drank it, toasted our feet in the glow of the hearth, and burned such quantum of tobacco, in cob pipes, that the walls seemed to melt away in the smoke. Mrs. Vignal, her feet on a hassock, knitted away quietly, and if she spoke at all it was to her daughter, who sat behind her in a chair, bent forward, listening to us, intently, and I wondered what she could find of interest in our talk of soil, plants, herbs, and so forth. But she laughed often, overeager, I thought, to find our talk amusing. It was quite noticeable. That gave me my cue. I gave an account of the queer things that had happened to me at the Jardin des Plantes, and in knocking around London. I laid on the color.

"She laughed, mirthfully. But I wished she had laughed without that sharp, hysterical undertone. Vignal smoked in content, nodding his head, but talking very little indeed, as if his mind were elsewhere, out in his garden, or at sea. He had no ready gift of speech, though his life had been full of strange experience. So I talked only for the girl. This was a holiday evening for her.

"At midnight the party broke up. Vignal went upstairs to get his best hat and coat, and his wife followed him, to pick out a warm muffler. That left me alone a minute with the girl.

" 'I hope you will come here often,' she said. 'Do come whenever you can. Do you know what it means to us—to me—to hear people laugh?' She gripped my wrist. Her eyes were wistful and pleading. 'For a long time after we came here to live, I thought I couldn't stand it. So please, Mr. Casson—'

" 'Assuredly I'll come,' I said. 'The very first time I'm this way again.'

"Her parents came down. I said good-by to her and the cheery Mrs. Vignal, and went out into the driveway. How refreshing was the air! The plants were quick with odor. Azaleas were heavy along the path, and there was a skirting of basils and salvia, and marjorams, their curly tops lolling like the heads of cherubim. I got into the car, and we drove off.

"Vignal was in easier mood on this drive, more of the host, more communicative. He had a lot to say of horticulture, though he spoke with hesitancy and an accent, and after a while lapsed into French. He was born in Dalecarlia, a farming region in Sweden, and reared there. It was a life that made a deep impression on him. He talked of the birds, the trees lashed by the wind, the immense storms, the harvests, and the old farmhouse with swallows' nests under the eaves. And when he was eighteen he went to sea.

" 'You have had enough sea life?' I asked.

" 'Too much. Nearly thirty years of it. Even when I was master I dreamed of the land. I could smell it leagues out at sea. I was drawn to it by a great longing that I cannot describe. Just as some men have a longing for the unseen and the eternal.

" 'And now I am upon it. What more can I ask? I have my trees and shrubs and grass to take care of. And there is the smell of the fresh earth. I am happy when I dig in it, when my spade cuts handily into the packed soil and rings sharp against the gravel. There is no smell like the incense of the upturned earth, the aroma of it when it is moist and deep under turf. When I dig in full sunlight, a steam rises, and butterflies dance in it as birds do in the spray of a fountain.

" 'No, I shall never weary of it. To me it is the breath of life itself. It is another wine. It goes to my head, and I could work in it all day and half the night.'

"He broke off to speak about his wife. He met her when he was at Havre during the war. He brought his wife to Baltimore, then became a citizen. Just a year now, it was, that he had been living out here in the country.

" 'She was very glad to see you,' he said. 'It is not often that she hears her own language.'

" 'For an exile she has done very well,' I remarked. 'And I am sure she is quite content.'

" 'Oh, yes.'

"He threw me a glance, then fell silent. I had it on the tip of my tongue to speak about the girl, but I knew what was going through his mind, and I refrained. So we talked about something else. I promised him I'd come again, if luck should bring me to Philadelphia once more. He said that he'd be on the lookout for me. Soon we were at the hotel, and, as it was late, our farewell was brief.

"I stayed in town only a day more. Going into a shop I bought some books I felt Dittany Vignal would like.

" 'And the address?' asked the clerk.

"I didn't know. It had been most negligent of me not to inquire. However, the clerk was obliging, and, with the one clue that the place was out in the country somewhere, hunted through the directory.

" 'I believe we have it now,' she said, looking up. 'There is a Mr. Vignal resident out at Woodmere. That is a cemetery, sir. And he is the caretaker.' "

XIII

Tinkers' Holiday

About this time I suddenly wearied of my way of life—of the heated kitchen, the smells of roasting meat, the sad, Dervish-like cries of the waiters, the intrigues of the under-chefs, the ephemeral nature of the work in hand, the endless voracity, the plaints of the same overstuffed clients night after night. Bread was good enough for them—bread and water! I loathed the sight of food. It is a malaise that frequently attacks chefs, and waiters. I had made the wrong choice of arts, and was now in black despair. I envied the tinker, and the pavior by the roadside, sitting under a hedge with his pipe, cracking stones with his long hammer, his luncheon of bread and an apple tied up in a red kerchief. Their crafts were humble, but they could see in a mended kettle that would long endure, or a length of smooth road that would outlast themselves, justification for their toil, and next morning behold the sun rise above another hill. In short, I was filled with ennui.

And there also had been Célie.

Célie sat at the marble counter by the door of the Roi Nantois, taking in the money and selling the cigars. Her upper lip was short and curled, her hair a coppery tumble. She was stout, and she was older than I. Three times in a month I had taken her to the cinema in the Rue de la Gaîté, and on her free days to the Luxembourg to hear the band music. It was an infatuation, but terrible while it lasted. We kissed often, in the doorway to her lodging, and I went reeling home under the stars, drunk of an insensate folly. François it was who brought me back more or less to my wits. He took me by the shoulders one night in the park, shook me until I was stupefied, and bellowed truth into my ears. My infatuation was the scandal of the Roi Nantois, and the jest of the dishwashers. Célie Duval was more than twice my age; she was uglier than Pierre; and a clandestine affair of one night was the utmost I could ever dream of for a reward, and that too was a hopeless dream, for she was not only the most grubbing of skinflints, but she was living with a station porter, who was to marry her after they had hoarded up, sou by sou, enough to buy a little café in Rouen. There was more, but I shall not add to my chagrin by setting it all down.

It takes more than a pitchfork to drive out passion. I do not know what would have become of me if the cauldron at the Roi Nantois had not sprung a leak. It was a sort of talisman, a large and ancient copper pot, perhaps two centuries old, with a rim carved in a design of acorns and leaves. In a couple of months when the tourist season began, it would be needed. I engaged a carter, and with this cupola of a pot drove out to a gypsy camp the other side of the forest at Fontainebleau. There are no repairers of pots like the gypsies, and I knew this tribe of coppersmiths, the Vascucci, who had come to the Roi Nantois a few times, and Tino, the head of the family, had once repaired a sugar boiler for my uncle in Provence.

Tino fell on my neck, so enchanted he was at seeing not only me but so handsome a pot. It was an hour's task for him to scratch about the leak the outline of a star—a six-pointed star, the coat of arms, the sign manual of the Vascucci—saw it out, fit in another star of copper, burnishing the hair-line joint so that the spelter shone like platinum. Then his two sons, and twenty gypsies from another camp, stood about, admiring the finished work.

"Jean-Marie," said Tino, in tearful pride, "do not go yet, for I must enjoy this masterpiece of cauldrons a whole hour to myself!"

Years of heat had, indeed, so dulled the ring of the cauldron when smitten that it gave forth a leaden sound. Tino squatted on the turf, lighted a pipe, upturned the cauldron, and swaged it all over with the flat of a mallet, so that after an hour it was singing like the matins bell in the tower of Saint Séverin. Down the road came another music: a Savoyard was playing his flute, and behind him was his wife trundling a handcart laden with adorable little Brieuc cheeses, while all about them capered their brown goats. It was a lovely, sunlit day, and linnets were singing madly in the beeches. The wind was blowing through the foliage and the telegraph wires as on an Aeolian harp. Tino lifted the cauldron into the cart.

"Where do you go now?" I asked, paying him the inadequate fee of thirty francs. "Toward the city?"

"We go South," said Tino. "Myself in this van, my two sons with the Gaspards, and three more vans of the Lavell family. South through the Auvergne, with its jam or biscuit works in every village, and as far as Arles, where they make nougats."

"Then I will come with you," I said, and sent the carter back home with the pot.

For two months with Tino and his group I traveled the road, *le grand jaspiner* of the French gypsies and the wandering showmen, a route so ancient that we came across cauldrons bearing signs and marks of tinkers whose families had died out a century before the Revolution. Those marks on pots, Tino read aloud for us, as if they were a book of history or inscriptions left on the walls of a cave by primitive man. The life in itself was admirable. We slept and ate in dens open only to the initiates of the road and the tan bark; or under hedges, dining on roast hedgehog, bread, and thistle greens—rough fare, but honestly gained, and seasoned well with hunger. With the gendarmes we got along on terms of self-respecting hostility. But no trouble befell us. Twice, perhaps, some of the Gaspards were locked up after the loss of somebody's goose, or for carrying a knife a mere hand's-breadth too long, and had to wait until Tino arrived to spring them.

Tino Vascucci had the knack of clearing up these embarrassing matters in no time at all. He had flowing mustachios, candid eyes, and the dignity of an Arab patriarch. There was the time I went with him to the police yard at Figeac, where his two sons and the Gaspards, a sturdy brood, lolling about under the trees, nonchalant, smoking, were awaiting us.

"Stealing a goose, you say?" he echoed, shocked to the boots. "Impossible!"

"But they were seen," insisted the commissioner. "One moment the goose was in the field, and next moment it was gone—and there these Bohemians driving down the street."

"That still proves nothing!" Tino cried out in triumph. "And, besides, these are rightly brought up young men, incapable of such trickeries! Now, if it were a horse, or a pair of oxen—one might understand. But a fowl, that would be illogical. And again, never in their lives have they been in trouble!" This was a flight of rhetoric, of course. Also it was but the beginning of Tino's declamation, which brought in a crowd from the street. "And to prove what admirable reputations these youths possess—behold!"

He would unfold a paper, always the same paper, for the gendarmes to scan, impressed, and to discuss with frowns and nods and twistings of their mustaches. Ten minutes more, for the sake of formality, and the Gaspards, the Vascucci, and myself would be driving down the street again, free as birds.

That paper always worked, and Tino kept it under his seat, ready for any emergency. I asked him what it was, and how he came by it.

"That young crew of originals, I could not get them out of jail without that paper!" chuckled Tino. "It always works the first time!

"I was going down the Rue Gambetta one day, and what should I see but a doorway hung with crape. I watched, and saw there was to be a funeral. Evidently, from all the gendarmes in the house, it was the funeral of a high police official. At the door was a little table with a condolence book on it, and it seemed all the gendarmes in Paris were writing their names in it.

"I am not one of any great education, Jean-Marie, but I have a respect for learning, though I can no more than count.

"So, when there was no one left about the door, I went over, made believe to write my name, but instead tore off a page and hid it under my cloak. Papa Gaspard, who is a scholar, that night read aloud the page. We fell upon each other's neck! A peculiar treasure had come into our hands—a passport full of good names. A mayor, two deputies, three bankers, police sergeants, and twenty gendarmes! There was a blank space on top, and on this Papa Gaspard wrote a little piece telling everyone what good and honest people the Vascucci are, and the Gaspards, and urging that all show them every manner of high consideration and politeness.

"It is a safe-conduct that has so far worked very well, like an incantation. As in that affair of the goose. But on the way back we may have to take another road."

I had written to François, and when we came to the inn of the Black Hen, at Orange, there was a reply awaiting me, urging me to return, adding that I was missed, and that Célie, having married her porter, had left. I sent him word that I would be back at the Roi Nantois in three weeks, after I finally got to Marseilles, saw the unveiling of the statue to Mistral, the poet of Provence, and dined with my friends of the road at the restaurant of Mère Blanchet. That latter was a treat I had promised myself, and a little return for the kindness they had shown me.

All the rest of the way down we dined *maigre*—on bread, a fish caught in the river, salad of grass, plucked in the field, and dressed with a little oil and the juice of a handful of unripe grapes. We lived sparely, like monks on a pilgrimage, and slept hard and long under the hedges, and work had us all under its spell. From Figeac to the Camargue we traversed a country rife with leaky pots and cauldrons and kettles, and Tino made everyone behave, for we were in a region of old and valued clients. Indeed, if a pot were distinguished, and of copper, Tino mended it himself, denying himself a glass of wine, no matter how great his desire, so that his hands, so skilled at wielding the little files, might be adequate to the task. Night after night he frugally supped on bread and water. "Why?" I asked him.

"Jean-Marie," he said, "I shall not dine until I sit with you at Mère Blanchet's table."

There was more wisdom in this old gypsy's finger than in all the steady patrons at the Roi Nantois, who were unaware that surfeit leads but to boredom. Tino was the true hedonist, aware that we cannot feast unless we are willing also to fast. No passion, no pleasure, no interest must be slaked at will. Indeed, to keep it sharp and alive, the wish to gratify it must often be denied, or else it become the foe of its own gratification.

We were driving out of the Camargue that night, when the moon was dim; young Basil Gaspard was riding with us for a change, and he had the reins. He pulled up, sniffed, and his eyes slid as he peered through the dark. I could see nothing but the lantern at the end of the shaft and the horses. Basil drew a long breath, his finger wavered, then pointed over the front wheel into the ditch.

"There!" he whispered. "An old one with some young!"

A scent lifted up to us, a scent as of celery leaves, licorice, and frost-bitten apples, all bruised underfoot: the unmistakable scent of live pork. Basil inhaled it deeply, his nose quivering; he tightened his belt, stood on the wheel, and poised, like a diver, with hands outstretched. He leaped into the darkness. There was a drum-like thwack, then a grunt. He had landed on a sow. The first note of a shriek rent the air, and it was choked off.

Basil came up with a grin, holding up a little pig, its legs flurrying like egg beaters.

"Look at him! A tender one, sweet as butter! How would he look in a pan, with a basketful of onions in him?"

"Like an angel," said Tino, scratching its head with his pipe stem. "Now you put him right back! That's right. Now you can jump in!"

We were all still fasting when we reached Marseilles that gala day, with a fair, a street carnival, and immense crowds on the Cannebière, and it seemed as if half of Provence had poured into the town to attend the dedication of the statue to the great Mistral. From where we sat in our carts we had a good view, and we heard all the speeches, the songs, and the music of the bands, with their brasses, tambours, and fifes, so infinitely moving to a Provençal exile like myself.

"*O Magali, ma tant amado. . . .*" Tino and I both sang Mistral's lyric as loudly as did the rest. The Mayor pulled at the cord, the canvas rose, disclosing to the eyes of the reverent the figure of the poet, high on the pedestal, arm held out rigidly, pointing toward the hills and his native *aillane*, with its gardens and cypresses.

It was inspiring, and such was the intent of the sculptor. But on the faces of some citizens about me was depicted a shocked embarrassment; the beard of one silk-hatted elder on the platform, who happened to be orating at the time, was trembling with suppressed mirth. The hand of the statue was pointing straight at an alley populated by the daughters of joy.

The poet, though I am not sure, for I haven't been to Marseilles in a long time, may have been turned since, to indicate its pride, the harbor.

Straight on to Mère Blanchet's we went, an old rendezvous of mine when I followed the sea; and we played cards and dominoes and drank wine until evening, when Mère Blanchet called us in to dinner—a very special dinner she had prepared for us. It was so special that she had laid the table with the one tablecloth in the house. It was old, of linen, heavily embroidered, an heirloom, and part of the dowry she had brought when she came down from Nantes, to marry Hippolite Blanchet, now gone. No other guests would she serve that night, or not with the elaborate dishes she had cooked for myself and my gypsy friends, who banqueted, as they had never before banqueted in their lives. And I had much to celebrate! My infatuation for Célie was gone! That called for champagne.

The other clients dined on ragout of hare, or tripe, on bare tables. Being kings, naught was too good for us. At midnight I requested my bill.

"Lobsters, birds, a roast, salads," Mère Blanchet muttered. "For eight, ten, let me see." She clapped a hand to her forehead, and counted aloud. The mental gymnastics were beyond her. With her thumbnail she marked on the tablecloth. "The fruits, the cheese, the coffee." She marked again. "And the cognac and the cigars." Adding up the marks twice, "Three hundred francs," she read.

I counted out the money, with another note for luck, and, after stuffing it under her apron, she reached for the cognac bottle to

give us a last round. A voice snarled out from among the card players. A hard-eyed gendarme, evidently no friend of gypsies, and who
had most probably dined on tripe and onions, was glaring at us.

"Mère Blanchet, it's time you respected the law for once! A bill
must be stamped. It must then be receipted, then given to your
client, whose property it is."

The poor woman was aghast, but she fetched a stamp from a box
above the mantelpiece, stuck it on the tablecloth, and wrote across
it. Then she handed a corner of the linen to me. I essayed, with
nonchalance, to stuff it into my pocket, then gave it up.

"Madame," I said, handing the corner back to her, "it is too large
a document for me to carry around, so please keep it for me until I
come around next time."

Her eyes were limpid with gratefulness, and we rose with our
glasses, and we drank our farewell round to her. It being nearly one
o'clock, I said good-by to the Vascuccis and the Gaspards, and rode
to the station, where I caught the express for Paris.

XIV

Lords and Ladies, *Vale!*

Louis of France decided to give a nuptial banquet in honor of a daughter of the powerful house of de Broglie. Cardinal Mazarin was to appear, and likewise the Prince de Condé, whom he had locked up tightly in jail for a brace of years. Since the bride was plain, overlarge, and bony, and had visited the altar twice before, and the groom was an obscure Seigneur, squat and unprepossessing, like the King-Frog in the fairy tale, the marriage struck no lyric note, and was possibly a marriage of convenience. Tongues were heard to say that the union interested Louis not at all, and that, weary of the bickering between the Cardinal and the Prince, he saw in the banquet a chance to bring them together for a reconciliation. It was not probable they would fight at the table. But many were curious. The crowned heads of three countries, and fur-wrapped envoys from Sweden, Muscovy, and Poland, traveling by ship, coach, or sledge, began to press earnestly along the route to Fontainebleau.

The importance of the wedding, as historians have since proved, was not illusory. Indeed, word had already got about that this was likely to be the last banquet of D'Aujac, the greatest chef in France. In his cell he had sat for days, composing the bill of fare. It was a work of splendor almost unprecedented, as stately as an oratorio by Handel. It was an epithalamium of wines, a processional of stags, cygnets, bustards, turbots, elaborate set pieces, fruits uncounted, desserts, and Sicilian ices—these last in compliment to the Cardinal, who was a Sicilian. The death of Mazarin was undeplored by Frenchmen, and D'Aujac, it is clear, had a low opinion of him. The apex of the feast was roast stag in pastry, with a sauce that the chef had invented for the occasion, and rightly he named it after himself, Sauce D'Aujac.

The banquet, with its dishes and wines and music on clarinets, had the grandeur of the Italian Renaissance, save that it unfolded more rapidly, with centuries packed into staggering hours. In the kitchen, at the precise moment, D'Aujac hobbled to the fires, leaning on the arm of an apprentice, for he was ninety-two, and an ague had rendered him infirm. The cooks followed, desirous to assist at the birth of the new dish—for it was nothing less, this sauce. There were some who noticed that the master seemed agitated, that his hand trembled. But his soul was resolute. In the pan, over hot coals, the wine, essences, and butter leaped to their fusion. In the supernal light of the torches, his voice rang as he called out for the ox palates, the bowl of Espagnol, the tray heaped with rods of marrow. They were cast in. Then he faltered; the spoon fell from his hand, and he collapsed.

"It is done!" he murmured, expiring like Pindar in the arms of his disciples. "Ah, D'Aujac, what the planet is losing in you!"

He had toiled overlong since youth, being insatiable of fame— no bad thing in itself, if it procure a man happiness, and without oppression of his fellow beings. But fame is not peace of mind, for ambition, vain and disturbing, is its mainspring.

That apprentice had a sharper ear than his fellows in the kitchen of Fontainebleau that night, and the words of the master were burned into his memory. He became a cook at a hunting lodge on the outskirts of Paris, and when, a hundred years later, it became the Roi Nantois, the Sauce D'Aujac was still a secret of the establishment.

Under the hand of François it acquired more dash, more brilliance, and a luster which the astute Boulestin praised, and attributed to a toning with a glaze from the neck meat of bulls. François said nothing of it. The *panache*, the dramatic quality of this Creole, was outward merely. He shrank from popular acclaim; there was lacking in him that egomania dashed with charlatanry, or scoundrelism, as often to be observed in the arts as in politics. Nor was he intolerant. Like Aristotle, he was a great epicure in respect of fish, and said that a bloater, caught off Yarmouth in November, and correctly fried, was as perfect a thing as Rembrandt's "The Night Watch," and that if France had a cheese to match the Stilton or a ripened Double Gloucester, he hoped somebody would tell him what it was.

In several ways François was the wisest chef in the long history of the Roi Nantois. He had contrived no new sauce or dish. Like the magisterial Chinese potters and weavers, who invent nothing, he was content to repeat the classic designs. Not originality but perfection is the lodestar of the virtuoso, who knows that a perfect work cannot be improved upon, and that it takes more skill and conscience to make a vibrant, living copy than to create a poor original.

It is Epicurean to reject glory and pleasures bought at too high a cost, and to hold that the *summum bonum* is to live pleasantly, unknown, in serenity and prudence, far from the era of conflict. François, in short, abdicated his throne at the Roi Nantois. It was on an Easter night, after a thousand dinners had been sent up, and in the sluggish air the staff, limp and fatigued, was falling out.

"Messieurs!"

There he stood, truncately massive and solemn, in the doorway of his office, crowned with the black toque that he wore only on state occasions. Near by was the *sommelier*, with chain and key, a cart before him, loaded with champagne and glasses. The staff came forward.

François spoke: "Messieurs, I have to speak to you directly, and I shall be brief. I have resigned, and I retire to the country. From all of you, my colleagues, I part with a grief that is inexpressible. Let me point to my successor, Jean-Marie Gallois!"

It was a surprise to everyone but myself. The cooks lifted a shout, and hammered on their ranges and tables with pots. The champagne was poured, and Urbain, lifting his glass, called out: "A double toast! To François and to Madame François!"

And that, too, was a surprise! It was like being told that one's bishop had not only given up his miter but had taken a lady to wife. There was clamor, and handshaking, a great pouring out of champagne, and a farewell that lasted an hour.

I walked home with François. He was in a poetic mood, and, emotionally giving himself thumps on the chest with his stick hand, talked only of the lady awaiting him at Aix-en-Provence.

"Our proprietors grieve at their loss," I said.

"They were shocked!" he admitted. "Profoundly!"

For all the austerity of his office and devotion to his exacting craft, François was no more immune to the tender passion than a tenor, a statesman, or an engineer of bridges. The renowned of the *haute cuisine* have been neglected by the artificers of romance. Playwrights have written moving dramas of a hero's sonata, statue, even of his nose, but never of a hero's sauce. Chanticleer had his Rostand, but what celebrator had a Vatel or a Carême to descant his achievements in drama, epic, or any prose above journalism? Vizetelly and Sala and Léon Daudet, pardon! They have so written, and with eloquence: the practitioners of one ephemeral art in tribute to another.

François had long courted this lady near Aix—a widow sought after by a hundred Romeos, no doubt; and well she might be, for she had a delicious large farm with a tangerine grove, cork and olive trees, a fishing pool, abundance of sheep, and pastures waist-deep in grass, rosemary, and tall, purple foxgloves. And he had triumphed. Or should one not say, knowing the widow, the amiable, large-girthed, and soft-eyed Yvette, so fond of exquisite foods, and knowing our François, that it was a triumph for the lady?

I visited them before I left France, saw that herb-redolent farm where François, clad on the Provençal horseman model, with russet velours and a wide hat, raised fine green melons as round as any Turk. Afternoons, he dressed to visit the café at the village, where he held forth with the Mayor, and shouted poetry as if he were Mistral or Jasmine the Barber.

He cooked no more, not anything, except now and then a crisp fish, a brace of guinea hens, or a gigot of mutton on Sunday, with some of those laudable haricots. "And then only, you understand, to please Yvette."

When I came he had gone up into the Alpilles, where the sheep had been taken to avoid the searing heat. The excitement of their return! Awakened by great sound of barking, I climbed out through the window. It was moonlight, and the nip of autumn was in the air. The house dogs bayed insanely in welcome, and the peacocks in the yews, their tulle crests like turbans against the moon, espied the flocks and hailed them with loud trumpetings. All I could see was an advancing surf of dust. Then came the shepherds, and in the rear François on a horse. It was a noble sight. Under those beeches had passed many popes, an emperor, fourteen monarchs of France, and Petrarch.

I went out with Yvette to greet him. He had a bucket of snails hung from his saddle, and a sack of wild partridge jumbled in sweet marjoram, thyme, and rosemary.

We had a picnic next day, on a wooded slope where we roasted the partridges in a fire of roots with the herbs, baked the snails, and from the brook, which ran icy cool and bathed the feet of his tangerine trees, we took out our chilled melons and a bottle of dry, flinty Crau wine. The shepherds joined us, and the mayor, and we dined in the rustic simplicity of the Golden Age. Tangerines scented the air; the crickets made it audible. The sunshine warmed our throats, and the flinty wine seemed cooler, and trickled down our gullets more gratefully than if it had been Yquem. We talked. Yvette, sloe-eyed and as large as a house, slumbered blissfully, her head on François' lap. We listened to the tinkle of the rams' bells as the flock began to graze their way up the hill. A shepherd untied a paper, took out a lump of glistening, veined jade—wild honeycomb that dripped as he broke it for us. We ate honey to the soft Thessalian music of bells jangled by the black-muzzled rams, whose fleece was like cotton-wool against the indigo of the sea below. They lapped in the water, the wool bearers; they cropped at the seared grass and thyme, releasing dust and the earth scent, combatting for blossom heads with the golden scarabs and bees. How fat they had all grown in the lush, green Alpilles!

"In the spring we shall have plenty of lambs," said the shepherd. "Surely, a hundred."

"My angel," said François, "behold! We are surrounded by gigots."

Yvette awoke and gazed about her, blinking in the sunlight. She popped a fragment of honey into her mouth. "Ah, the little gamins," she cried, wiping her fingers on a fleece. "Listen to them bleat. They want to trot right into the ovens."

It is doubtful, said Epicurus, if marriage has helped any man, and one may be well content if it does him no harm. Did he grave it on his tablet after dining on honey and partridge with shepherds, and with a sleepy shepherdess pillowed on his knee?

———

Bon fruit murit tard, affirm the old gardeners, distrustful in their wisdom of fruit and men of early ripenings. Perhaps I had matured too early. In the gloom of their despair—for had not the prestige of the Roi Nantois evanesced with the stocky François?—the owners thrust me into the post of *chef de cuisine*. They could not have marveled more than I that the vessel kept afloat. And yet, somehow, it advanced.

Did not the Club des Cent, that hierarchy of gastronomes, banquet twice in our Louis XIV salon? Did not Pierre think it a poor, a dreadful, night if Prosper Montagne, M. Boulestin, or André Simon, or Ali Bab were not dining at the honor table near the Venetian glass mirror? The garden adjoining was taken over and roofed with lattice for a supper Belvedere. It flourished so that Pierre, now mysteriously one of the sharers in the firm, made it a jungle of palms, whose glazed fronds caressed the ear and the tiara. One may not, to paraphrase Goethe, dine with impunity beneath palms; for the fiber weakens, and the palm lover never asks the best music, and objects little, if at all, to paying out double for a dish or a wine, but the Roi Nantois, though it deplored the vegetation, ramped him not a sou the more.

We were also eclectic. We raided the great Democracy of the West, drawing upon it for Oysters Biltmore, the Gumbo Bisque, and a wine or two, notably, a leonine Zinfandel, grown near the Golden Gate of California. If America is in the main a gastronomical Sahara, it has its five delectable oases.

The Roi Nantois is still renowned; it still has masters in the kitchen. Gray and cheerful men with an affection for their tasks: acolytes of the *haute cuisine*, who have a reverence for the simple fruits of the earth, for honest vintners and makers of cheese, paste and sausages and conserves, for pressers of good oil, and a gratitude for birds and the dumb creatures, our link with the vegetable kingdom, who so meekly bow their heads to the pole axe. Heller, Pichon, Laplanche, Aubrey-Zay, all you in white bonnets—*vale!* I learned much from you, my masters!

In a year I began to weary of high post and glory.

I was, in pocket, richer than my old masters at the range. The good Baroness, that old friend of my uncle, had gone forth and peddled Nougat Masséna. Not, let me assure you, from door to door with a basket. She opened a villa at Cap Ferrat, and with excellent dinners worked up a background in the imposing grand manner. Brokers, warehousemen, and shop-chain owners who played roulette with her at the casino, and who progressed to a state of mellow feeling over her port, were so vulnerable that she inveigled them into buying Nougat Masséna by the ton, by carloads. They were extremely fortunate. It was good nougat, and it sold from the Bosphorus to Fifth Avenue.

I relinquished my share in the nougat factory to her. *Noblesse oblige,* and she had once done me a good turn. Besides, the sum she paid, though reasonable, was large. Judging from the size of it, she must have been desirous to consolidate her emotional attachment to the Establissement Masséna with a business link that took care of all the *convenances.* For quite a while now my uncle had been wearing a coat and usually passed as "M'sieu le Baron."

"Not at all a bad coup," Melun-Perret remarked as we were dining one night Chez l'Annamese. "What, may I ask, do you intend to do with that sickeningly large sum?"

"Roumanian oil?"

"Do nothing so imbecilic. That's my game."

"Well, then, it's already sunk in Guido's new place on Long Island."

Guido had done too well, for his restaurant had reached that deplorable phase of success when patrons came in not so much to eat as to be seen. It was a mockery of success. The cuisine, the wines, the chef were subordinate to the clientele—jazz nabobs, film players, and so forth. Melun-Perret listened in agony.

"He's retiring farther inland," I went on, "miles and miles. So far that patrons will have no motive to go there except to eat gratefully at famine prices."

"I would have been good for an unreasonable sum," he muttered cloudily. "But if, later—" He drummed on the table vacantly, and looked at the sleet-trickled window. "Damned sorry. So many old friends dropping off like this. Where do you leave from?"

"I don't know. Havre, perhaps."

"No." He shook his head firmly. "Decidedly not. In a week or so I'll be running through Spain. Because of the war. Why not ride on with me to Barcelona?"

I thought of Freda and, much less, of Rémy, who had a hand on a chain of hotels in the Peninsula. I pitched a coin. Heads it was.

"Why not?" I said.

All the next week Aragon and Castille were about us. We crawled slowly through the tawniness and desolation of Spain, by caprice and starts, generally at night, and often to be waked by the thumping of rifle butts on the door. The armed guards could not always see the bunting at the ends of the train. Burgos closed behind us with a barrier of steel, for we were the last train out; and the train was all Melun-Perret's. He had some vague, discretionary powers from Governments. His was the unreal sphere of intrigue, diplomacy, and high finance that transcends boundaries. The train itself—engine and a salon coach marked with a crest under gilt festoons—was a reality. Quite as much was it a dream. We had a library and shower bath, a valet, and Ramon, the chef. We had safe conduct; we were persons of importance; and we were headed inflexibly, whatever might fall, for Barcelona. It was a train with the stopping instinct well developed. Visitors had slipped in and out all the way from the border.

A telegram came to him as we were sitting in the library. Georges looked out into the rain. His cigar went out. He relighted a fresh one, and it died in his fingers. Overhead droned a plane, following the rails.

"It is far worse, far worse, than they thought," he said. He flicked his thumb upward. "I shall have to fly back on that. And you stay on. Take your time."

He packed a grip and a portfolio. "I am sorry I shall miss dinner with you. Our last dinner in a long while, Jean-Marie. Drink to your friends in the old, dark Rioja. *Adios!*"

A last handshake, and he was gone. Madrid next, and we slid into a yard on its outskirts. It was pitch-dark. I dispatched a telegram to Freda, then engaged a taxicab at a ransom.

The house, towering and gloomy, like a small version of the Escurial, was dimly lighted. A servant unchained the door and admitted me.

"The Señora will be down in a moment."

He brought me cigarettes and a glass of sherry. I took a chair in a large *salle d'attente,* and smoked, staring at the broad, high staircase rising at the far end of the room, the flight of it cut halfway by the edge of the balcony under which I sat.

Had she remembered me after all these years? I asked myself. It was all so far back in the past when we were more than friends, when we were at school at Beynac's, and when I gave her a ring. Had we married, she would have known less of the luxury of which she was fond, and been the wife of an inn-keeper on the Rhone—a sleepy inn, with beehives, geraniums, and cabbages in the garden, and a sign creaking in the breeze.

A rustle atop the stairway, and I saw a pair of jet slippers. Slowly they descended, step by step. It was Freda descending, and my eyes traveled up her gown, to the edge of her fan, then to her hand. Upon her finger shone a ring with a large emerald, and it was visible and shining as she held out her hands, and I went to meet her.

"Jean-Marie!"

"Freda!"

The past enfolded us, and for hours we sat talking, laughing, falling into silences, talking again. Then I rose to bid her good-by.

"Rémy will be sorry to have missed you," she said. "And if he were here, you could travel together. He had to leave, and I am sure that friends of his, who have a car, could have taken you both as far as Saragossa, if no farther. A day or two there, and you might again find a way out."

She accompanied me to the door. It was dark, the night smelled of rain, and there was the rumble of cannon, with glare on the horizon.

"Stay, Jean-Marie. All the roads are closed but one. You see, we are as good as besieged. And there are simply no trains going out. Rémy tried, but could find none."

"There is one," I said. "It is waiting for me at the siding. A private train. I am sorry Rémy has already left, for I could take him wherever he wants to go."

The look she flung at me—the look of wonder, of uncertainty—lightened the pain I had felt for eight long years.

"Oh—I didn't know—" she said. "*Adios,* then, Jean-Marie!"

I had no time for explanation, for I was scrambling into the taxi-cab. It hurtled into the darkness, and in twenty minutes, after detouring many barricades, I was at the station. The armed guards thrust me up the steps, and, as they followed, one turned to point up into the sky.

Precisely then the aerial bombardment started. There was a drumming, as of a child's rattle grotesquely magnified. The night was scratched with bright zigzags, was loud with whistlings that burst into red detonations. Then the metal keys to heaven and hell opened their diapason with notes that echoed and flowered in the clouds. Somewhere in the yard a bomb jarred on the earth, and the uproar was like the explosion of a comet in a boilerworks as engines and rails were twisted into a wire puzzle.

"If the Señor will be seated," said the butler, pointing to the table. "Dinner will be served him."

I had not dined. I was in no mood for dining. But Ramon came in, bearing a haunch of boar smoking on a platter. The dark Rioja was on the cloth, a magnum of it. Just then fists thumped on the side of the coach.

"Open the door," I said to the guard. "Let them in, let them all in. Hurry!"

Out of the night ten piled in—soldiers and yard workmen, one tying up a bleeding wrist. No more entered, though we called and shouted into the night as the train moved out of range, with blinds pulled down.

"A dinner for twelve," I said to Ramon.

Chairs and folding stools we dragged to the table. Ramon ignited the brandy, and spooned fire and sauce over the haunch. He bent pridefully over it, flicking herbs into the blaze, unheeding of the nerve-wracking thunder about us in a world gone mad. Art is enduring. Madness comes and goes, as it ever will. The artichokes were succulent, the salad cool in a frosted silver bowl.

I poured out the Rioja—a brimming glass for everyone. We all stood up.

"Tonight, *amigos,* we shall eat and drink and make mirth. Tomorrow—"

Only the present is ours, said Epicurus.

A NOTE ON THE TYPE

The principal text of this Modern Library edition
was set in a digitized version of Janson,
a typeface that dates from about 1690 and was cut by Nicholas Kis,
a Hungarian working in Amsterdam. The original matrices have
survived and are held by the Stempel foundry in Germany.
Hermann Zapf redesigned some of the weights and sizes for Stempel,
basing his revisions on the original design.